# A2 Music
# Revision Guide

GW00545543

# Sally Ellerington

**R• RHINEGOLD
EDUCATION**

www.rhinegoldeducation.co.uk

**Music Study Guides**
GCSE, AS and A2 Music Study Guides (AQA, Edexcel and OCR)
GCSE, AS and A2 Music Listening Tests (AQA, Edexcel and OCR)
AS/A2 Music Technology Study Guide, Listening Tests and Revision Guide (Edexcel)
Revision Guides for GCSE (AQA, Edexcel and OCR), AS and A2 Music (Edexcel and OCR)

**Also available from Rhinegold Education**
Key Stage 3 Listening Tests: Book 1 and Book 2
AS and A2 Music Harmony Workbooks
GCSE and AS Music Composition Workbooks
GCSE and AS Music Literacy Workbooks
Romanticism in Focus, Baroque Music in Focus, Modernism in Focus, *The Immaculate Collection* in Focus,
*Who's Next* in Focus, *Batman* in Focus, *Goldfinger* in Focus, Musicals in Focus
Music Technology from Scratch
Understanding Popular Music

First published 2012 in Great Britain by
Rhinegold Education
14–15 Berners Street
London W1T 3LJ

www.rhinegoldeducation.co.uk

© Rhinegold Education 2012
a division of Music Sales Limited

All rights reserved. No part of this publication may be reproduced, stored in a retrieval system, or transmitted in any form or by any means, electronic, mechanical, photocopying, recording or otherwise, without the prior permission of Rhinegold Education.

Rhinegold Education has used its best efforts in preparing this guide. It does not assume, and hereby disclaims, any liability to any party for loss or damage caused by errors or omissions in the guide whether such errors or omissions result from negligence, accident or other cause.

You should always check the current requirements of the examination, as these may change.
Copies of the OCR specification can be downloaded from the OCR website at www.ocr.org.uk or may be purchased from OCR Publications, PO Box 5050, Annersley, Nottingham, NG15 0DL.
Telephone: 0870 870 6622     Email: publications@ocr.org.uk

**OCR A2 Music Revision Guide**
Order No. RHG207
ISBN: 978-1-78038-244-9

Exclusive Distributors:
Music Sales Ltd
Distribution Centre, Newmarket Road
Bury St Edmunds, Suffolk IP33 3YB, UK

Printed in the EU

# Contents

## The author

Sally Ellerington is a graduate of Trinity College of Music and taught for thirty years at Monmouth Comprehensive School where she led a large team of class and visiting instrumental teachers. She has experience of preparing large groups of students for GCSE and A-level Music. She has been involved in curriculum development for Key Stage 3 and A Level and is currently a senior examiner at A level.

## Copyright

Excerpt from "A Sea Symphony"
Music by Ralph Vaughan Williams
© Copyright 1918 Stainer & Bell Ltd, London, England.
Reproduced by permission.
All Rights Reserved. International Copyright Secured.

# Introduction

For the OCR A2 qualification in music you have to complete three units:

- G354 Performing Music 2: Interpretation (40% of the total A2 mark)
- G355 Composing 2 (30% of the total A2 mark)
- G356 Historical and Analytical Studies in Music (30% of the total A2 mark)

Success in any sort of examination is all about effective preparation. This revision guide will set out what is required and will support you in gaining the skills needed to achieve the best possible marks. The guide will mainly help you revise for the written examination, G356, but it also gives advice on G354 and G355, which you may not yet have completed.

## AREAS OF STUDY

All the work you complete for the A2 qualification is linked to two Areas of Study:

- Tonality
- Interpretation.

### TONALITY

AS level gave you a foundation in the basics of western tonal harmony. At A2 your understanding of tonality should build on this through:

- The stylistic technique exercises you complete for Composing 2
- Accompanied vocal music between 1900–1945 and the prescribed works and related repertoire you are studying for the Historical and Analytical Studies examination.

Make sure you are really comfortable with all the basics of harmony and tonality that you studied for AS level, so that you can develop a good understanding of the more complex harmonies and tonal processes that you find at A2 level. You may also encounter music which is not strictly tonal – for example it may be **atonal** or **modal**. For the purpose of your A2 course you should take tonality to include all forms of harmony, and the relationship between pitches in their widest sense.

### INTERPRETATION

You will demonstrate your understanding of interpretation through:

- Your performance recital and discussion with the examiner
- Your own composition to a chosen stimulus
- Your work on how other composers have interpreted a stimulus in the Historical and Analytical Studies paper.

Further details of what is required are given in the relevant sections of this guide.

# Unit G354 Performing 2: Interpretation (120 marks)

## WHAT IS REQUIRED?

- Section A Recital (100 marks) of up to 15 minutes in length consisting of pieces closely linked by style and genre (the 'focus').
- Section B Viva voce (20 marks) in which you discuss with the examiner different interpretations of music related to your recital focus and how these have influenced your own performing decisions. You will outline your research and findings on the viva voce preparation form, which will be given to the examiner on the day of the exam.

Both sections of the exam will be recorded. An audience can be present for the recital if you wish.

## TIPS FOR PREPARATION

By the time you read this book you will probably have chosen your recital focus and repertoire and have done preparatory listening for the viva voce, so these tips concentrate on the weeks leading up to the exam and the day itself.

- Practise carefully, especially all the passages you find difficult, but also ensure you play your whole recital as a 'performance' on several occasions before the exam. This is particularly important to build up stamina, but will also help you to gain confidence in dealing with nerves or unexpected slips in your performance. Play to an audience if you can.
- Photocopy your recital music in good time. Your teacher will need to send it to the examiner at least a week before the exam. Make sure it all fits on the page and mark in where you are omitting repeats and so on. If you have changed anything, mark this as well, so the examiner knows your intentions.
- Practise with your accompanist or ensemble members preferably in the room that will be used for the exam. Think carefully about balance between the parts.
- If you are a pianist, practise on the instrument you will use on the day.
- If your performance will be amplified, check the levels carefully. The volume must be suitable for the room used for the exam. It is your responsibility to know how to set up the equipment correctly, so if you are using unfamiliar gear make sure you know how it works.
- Complete your viva voce preparation form. It is worth spending the time needed to do this thoroughly because it will help you to discuss the music in depth when you are in the exam. Check you have included a bibliography with details of your background research. You will need a copy for the examiner and one for yourself. You can refer to your copy in the exam when you are talking to the examiner.
- Practise the viva voce with a teacher or friend. Use your instrument or voice to demonstrate points more clearly where appropriate.
- The night before the exam make sure you have everything ready – instrument, music, copies of the viva voce preparation form – and try to get a good night's sleep.
- Arrive in good time for the exam and ensure your accompanist and any ensemble members know what time they need to be there.
- Re-read the viva voce preparation form, so its details are fresh in your mind.

- Tune your instrument carefully before you go into the exam and check the tuning once in the exam room.
- Try to relax and enjoy yourself!

# Unit G355 Composing 2 (90 marks)

## WHAT IS REQUIRED?

- Section A Stylistic Techniques (45 marks) – a set of no more than eight exercises based on one style. One of the exercises must be completed in 90 minutes under centre supervision.
- Section B Composition (45 marks) – up to 4 minutes in length and based on one of:
  - a vocal setting of a text
  - an instrumental interpretation of a programme
  - music for film/TV.

## TIPS FOR PREPARATION

This unit is completed as coursework, so by the time you read this book you will probably have completed most of the exercises and be well on the way to finishing your composition. These tips concentrate on preparation for the centre-supervised exercise and the content of the final portfolio.

### THE SUPERVISED EXERCISE

- It is likely that you will complete the supervised exercise near the end of your course. Get plenty of practice at managing your time so that you use the full 90 minutes effectively. At the end of the 90 minutes there will be no opportunity to amend or improve the work.
- Revisit the exercises you have already completed and note any comments your teacher has given so that you avoid any errors you have made previously.
- You will have access to a keyboard or other instrument of your choice and you may also use a computer (but not plug-ins or other tools to aid working on the exercise).

### THE PORTFOLIO

- Work consistently during the course; don't leave everything to the last moment.
- Have everything ready in plenty of time before the deadline.

Your portfolio must consist of the following:

- Exercises – make sure each exercise is dated and has your name on it. Put the exercises in chronological order. Make sure your work is as neat as possible and that it is clear which parts were given and which you have added. Check your exercises carefully to ensure they are as accurate and stylistically idiomatic as possible.
- Composition – full score or a detailed commentary on the methods of mixing and producing your master recording. Present your score as accurately and clearly as you can.

- Recording – live or synthesised/sequenced. Allow enough time to make this as effective as possible so that it demonstrates your musical intentions. The CD you submit must work on normal stereo systems, so check yours carefully.
- Brief and commentary – make your brief clear and to the point. Include the text, translations or other visual stimuli you have used. Write about the composing process, incorporating details of how any existing music has influenced you. Then write a short appraisal of how well the composition fulfilled your brief. Check your spelling, punctuation and grammar. The brief and commentary are important because they inform the examiner about what you set out to do and what processes you followed to complete your composition.

# Unit G356 Historical and Analytical Studies in Music (90 marks)

## WHAT IS REQUIRED?

- Section A Aural Extract. Questions on an extract of accompanied vocal music written in the period from 1900 to 1945 (40 marks).
- Section B Historical Topics. Two essays from the prescribed topics (2 × 25 marks).

## ABOUT THE EXAMINATION

- The exam is available in January and June each year. The exact dates vary, so check with your school or college or on the OCR website (www.ocr.org.uk).
- The exam lasts for 1¾ hours plus 15 minutes preparation time in which you can listen to the extract, follow the score and read the question paper, but you may not write.
- Your paper will be externally marked by OCR examiners.
- Before the start of the exam you will be given:
  - The question paper – inside it will be the insert (the musical score for Section A)
  - The answer booklet
  - Manuscript paper
  - An audio CD.
- You will need to provide:
  - Pens and pencils
  - CD player and headphones, if your school/college is not providing them.

## THE LAYOUT OF THE PAPER

- The first page gives all the usual details about the exam, and there are also spaces for you to write your centre number, candidate number and your name. Write these clearly using capital letters for your name.
- On the next three or four pages will be the questions for Section A with spaces for your answers.

- After this will be the essay titles for Section B. There will be three questions for each topic. You must answer two questions from this section. Write your answers in the answer booklet. Make sure you fill in your details clearly on the first page and remember to write the number of each question at the start of your answer.
- If you use the manuscript paper to write musical quotations for Section B, write your details at the top of this sheet too. Remember to cross-reference the quotation in your essay.
- The music for Section A is contained in a separate insert. You do not need to write your details on this as it is not sent to the examiner, but you may make notes on it to help you answer the questions.
- At the end of the exam fasten together the question paper, answer booklet (together with any additional sheets) and manuscript paper. It is helpful to the examiner if you fasten them in the order given without putting anything inside the question paper.

## TOP TIPS FOR G356 (THE WRITTEN PAPER)

### SECTION A

- When you practise Section A questions get used to using the 15 minutes preparation time.
- Spend enough time on the longer questions in Section A (those that attract 6 to 10 marks) to give yourself an opportunity to show the examiner what you are capable of. Practise writing concisely but in detail about short passages of music.
- Read each question carefully and make sure you only refer to the bars of the music which are required.
- Try to keep your answer within the space given in Section A. If you have to continue in the answer booklet, make sure you write a note to say that is what you have done and label the question properly in the answer booklet.
- In order to do well in the comparison question at the end of Section A, revise some of the vocal music written between 1900 and 1945 that you have studied. The question will ask you to compare stylistic features of the examination extract with other music, so you will need to know some examples from this repertoire well.

### SECTION B

- Practise hand-writing Section B essays. Find a pen that allows you to write easily at speed. Remember you should use black ink for the examination.
- Revise carefully before writing practice timed essays. You need to know how much you can write in 30 minutes when you are really confident about your subject knowledge.
- Learn passages of music from the prescribed and related repertoire thoroughly. Make sure you can precisely identify the movement, song, scene or whatever. Remember you will be asked about the areas of study Tonality and Interpretation.
- Learn the spellings of composers, titles of repertoire and key musical words.
- Answer the specific question that is set. Keep your essay relevant. Do not waste time just writing everything you know.

# Making the most of this book

This revision guide deals in detail with Unit G356 Section A (pages 11–40) and Section B (pages 41–63), showing what you need to do, what the examiner is looking for and giving tips on how to improve your marks.

Read through each section of the book, working through the exercises as you come to them. Then revisit any areas which you feel need further attention.

# Preparing for G356 Section A: Aural Extract

## What is required

In Section A, you are required to answer questions based on an extract of **accompanied vocal music** written between **1900 and 1945**.

You will be provided with a CD recording and insert as well as the question paper.

## CD RECORDING

- The CD will consist of an audio recording of the extract and will also contain spoken information about the examination and the number of tracks used for the music. At A2 the extract will often be just one continuous track, but this is not always the case.
- You, or your school/college, will need to provide a CD player for your individual use in the examination. It should have a scan facility and a display so that you can use the timings given in the examination paper to help you.
- You should ensure that you are familiar with how to work the CD player you will use in the examination so that you do not waste precious time trying to find out how to operate the equipment.
- If you are using your own personal CD player, you should use fresh batteries and have some spares available.

## INSERT

- This consists of a score of the music for the extract.
- The vocal parts will be given in their entirety.
- The accompaniment will usually be on two staves. If the accompaniment is for piano, this will be complete. If the accompaniment is for another instrumental ensemble or orchestra, it will be printed as a reduction which shows the main features of the music.
- Bar numbers will be given at the start of each system.
- You may write on the insert if you want to make notes on the questions, but it will not be sent to the examiner and will not be marked, so make sure all your answers are written in the appropriate place on the question paper.

## QUESTION PAPER

- You are required to answer ALL the questions in Section A.
- Spaces will be provided for you to write your answers.
- The rubric (information) at the beginning of Section A will tell you the title of the music and the name of the composer. It will also set the text into context.
- The text of the extract will be printed as a block, together with a literal translation if the text is not in English.

- Each question will indicate which bars of the extract you should consider. You will also be given the track timings to match. For example:
  'What vocal textures are found in bar 20 to bar 33 (⊙ 0'53" to 1'24")?'
- In some questions you will find the beat of the bar indicated: for example, bar 20³ meaning bar 20 beat 3.
- The questions will be based around the two areas of study: Interpretation and Tonality. You will be assessed on your understanding of these aspects of the extract.

## Managing your time effectively

- The examination is 1 hour 45 minutes in length plus 15 minutes preparation time.
- During the preparation time, you are allowed to look at the question paper and the insert and to listen to the extract, but you must not write.
- Answers to Section A should be written in the spaces provided on the question paper.
- Answers to Section B should be written in the answer booklet.
- Remember the weighting of the paper:
  - Section A – 40 marks
  - Section B – 50 marks
- You are advised to spend about 45 minutes on Section A and 1 hour on the two essays in Section B. This may not seem long to complete the essays, but you will be writing about music which you have studied in depth, whereas in Section A the music will be unfamiliar.

### USING THE PREPARATION TIME

It is vital that you make good use of the 15 minutes preparation time. The time is given for you to familiarise yourself with the extract and the layout of the paper and insert so that you are ready to start answering the questions when the writing time starts. The extract itself will be up to 5 minutes in length.

> #### NOTE
>
> You might want to begin by turning to Section B in the question paper, finding the questions on the topic(s) you have studied and *briefly* considering which two you will answer – do NOT waste time on this: if you have prepared properly, you should have a choice of questions.

The following is a suggested plan for using the time wisely:

- Turn to Section A in the question paper and read the information about the extract that will be written at the start. This will put the music into context.
- Read through the text to get some feel for the meaning of the subject matter that the composer has set. Look as well at how the text is laid out – is it a poem in separate stanzas, for example? Is it dialogue to be performed by different voices? This might be an indication of how the music is structured. If there is a word or two that you do not understand, do not worry; when you listen to the music everything will probably become clearer. (3 minutes)
- Now listen to the extract, carefully following the score in the insert. (5 minutes)

- Read through the questions just to get a flavour for the sorts of things you are being asked. The first question usually concerns bars near the start of the music with subsequent ones working towards the end, though there might be one question which requires you to consider the extract as a whole. (2 minutes)
- If you have time, listen to the whole extract again; otherwise, listen to the section of the music needed for Question 1. (5 minutes)

## NOTE

Make sure that when you practise Section A questions you also get used to using the preparation time.

## How to prepare for Section A

- Read the section from pages 13–24 carefully, paying particular attention to the *Tips to improve your mark* on pages 18, 19, 20, 22 and 23. These will help you get to grips with the different musical aspects required for each question.
- Listen to some of the pieces you have studied for Section A and complete the exercises on pages 20, 21, 22 and 24.
- Study the practice questions on pages 24–40. These will help you get a feel for what, and how much, you need to write in the examination.
- Practise Section A questions by working through past papers – your school or college may have these – and by completing the exercises in Rhinegold's *OCR A2 Music Listening Tests* by Veronica Jamset.

## Approaches to different types of question

### LAYOUT

- Each question will be printed with blank lines for your answer underneath. There is usually one more line than the number of marks for each question or part question, though this is sometimes extended if there are several points to be made. You should aim to complete your answer within the space provided (see tips below). If you need to continue in the answer booklet, label the question correctly and make sure you indicate on the question paper that your answer continues.
- Most questions will refer to particular bars in the music. It sounds obvious, but make sure that you restrict your answer to consideration of these bars. Every year candidates waste time writing about bars that are not within the confines of the question. You will not gain marks for any answer which does not relate to the question, however inspirational that answer might be! You might find it helpful to mark on the insert the bars referred to in the question.
- There is often one question that splits into sections (a), (b) and (c). Such questions usually refer to the same bars, and these will be indicated at the start. For example:
  Q1   In bar 1 to bar 12 (⊙ 0'00  to 0'32 ):
  a.   Discuss the vocal textures. (3)
  b.   How does the accompaniment contribute to the mood? (4)

c. Discuss the expressive use of harmony and tonality. (3)
The blank lines for your answer will be after each part question. Make sure that you only write about the specified bars.

## QUESTION TYPES

Exactly which questions occur will depend on the nature of the musical extract, but the questions will focus on a range of features of the music. Aspects will include:

- Melodic devices
- Vocal/choral devices
- Structure
- Instrumental accompaniment
- Word painting
- Harmony and tonality
- How the music interprets the text
- Creation of mood
- Interpretation by the performers
- Comparison with another example of vocal music from the period 1900–1945.

You will need to be able to answer questions on all of these aspects and confident in using appropriate technical vocabulary to support your response. Pages 17–18 give you more detail about the different aspects, as do the practice questions at the end of this chapter.

## EFFECTIVE USE OF THE INSERT

You may find it useful to make notes on the insert, especially to mark the relevant sections for each question and maybe when identifying chords and keys. Make sure you listen carefully as you follow the music – there might be extra things happening that are not printed in the score. Remember that the examiner will not see anything you write on the insert as it is not sent to be marked.

## HOW MUCH TO WRITE AND HOW THE MARKS ARE DIVIDED

- You should be guided by the amount of space that has been given for your answer on the question paper and by the number of marks available for each question or part question.
- It is important for you to consider exactly what the question is asking and to decide what will be appropriate in your response before you start writing.
- Questions begin with a variety of key words. Make sure you take note of these, as understanding of what each requires will help you improve your mark. The table opposite provides guidance on key words:

| Key word(s) | Might refer to aspects such as | Marks and how much to write |
|---|---|---|
| Identify | instruments, voices, chords, keys | One-word answers are usually appropriate |
| Describe | vocal/instrumental textures, mood, structure | One mark for each correct response – a phrase is often needed rather than a single word |
| Explain | expressive use of tonality and harmony, changes of mood | Here you will only gain marks if you give some explanation; just stating a fact is not enough |
| Identify and explain | vocal/instrumental textures, expressive use of tonality, word painting | Usually one mark for each appropriate identification and one mark for a relevant explanation |
| Discuss | expressive use of tonality and harmony, changes of mood, interpretation of text – often used when a more extended musical passage is referred to in the question | Usually one mark for each relevant response if the question total is up to 6 marks; a holistic mark scheme is often adopted for questions worth more marks – see page 16 |
| Comment on | features of performance interpretation, effectiveness of certain features | Usually one mark for each relevant response if the question total is up to 6 marks; a holistic mark scheme is often adopted for questions worth more marks – see below |
| Show how | specific features of short passages | Usually one mark for each appropriate response |
| Compare | stylistic features, harmony and tonality in another vocal work from the period 1900–1945 | Holistic mark scheme – see page 16 |

- Each question will refer to particular bars of the extract. The bars will have been chosen to give you ample opportunity for an appropriate response, so make sure you consider the whole passage referred to. Although you will not need to write about *every* bar, there might be some obvious points to be made about the music later in the passage – this is often the case where harmony and tonality are involved, so don't get held up over a couple of difficult bars and miss easy marks from later on.
- There is no need to write in full sentences in Section A. Bullet points or brief statements are fine. The examiner needs to know how much you understand about the music so stick to the point of the question. Long, flowery explanations are unlikely to gain more marks.
- Correct use of technical musical terminology will help. One correct term can often save a whole phrase of generalised explanation and could even gain more marks.

# THE HOLISTIC MARK SCHEME

While some questions are worth a few marks (say 3 to 6) others will attract a higher number of marks. These questions are frequently more searching and require a detailed answer about a longer passage of music. For these questions examiners often use what is called a holistic mark scheme. This is one in which, instead of there being one mark per correct response, the examiner will read your answer and place it in the appropriate part of the mark scheme when awarding the mark.

The mark scheme below is similar to one that might be used for Sample Extract 2, Question 3 (page 38). Study it carefully and then note the points which follow:

| 9–10 marks | Answers demonstrate assured and precise aural perception by explaining in detail specific examples of how the music enhances the text in aspects of rhythm, word painting and orchestration. |
| --- | --- |
| 7–8 marks | Answers demonstrate assured aural perception by explaining in detail specific examples of how the music enhances the text in at least two of the required aspects. |
| 5–6 marks | Answers contain specific examples of how the music enhances the text, but lack detail of explanation, or refer in detail to only one aspect. |
| 3–4 marks | Answers refer to examples of how the music enhances the text, but fail to explain successfully. |
| 1–2 marks | Superficial observation only, with no explanation. |
| 0 marks | No relevant observations made. |

- You must give an appropriate answer to all aspects of the question to gain full marks.
- You must give detailed explanations to gain full marks.
- You need to *listen* carefully to the music, not just write about what you can *see* in the score.
- Make sure you write about features that are relevant to the question.
- You should listen to the relevant passage and choose appropriate examples that you can write about in detail, rather than writing vaguely about every bar.

## NOTE

Remember that 8 or 10 marks is $\frac{1}{5}$ or $\frac{1}{4}$ of the marks for the whole of Section A, so you should spend enough time on such questions (probably 10 or more minutes) to give yourself an opportunity to show the examiner what you are capable of.

Examples of the holistic mark scheme used for the final comparison question are given in the practice questions at the end of this chapter (page 39).

The pages which follow detail the areas you will be expected to respond to and the technical language you'll need to use.

# Musical features

These are the musical tools and devices that the composer has used to create the music. Thorough understanding of how the music is put together and confident use of the appropriate terminology to describe it are essential to gain a high mark.

The particular terms you will need to use in the examination will depend, of course, on the nature of the extract, but you should know the meaning of all the following technical vocabulary and be able to apply it appropriately.

Many of these terms will be ones you already understand and you might find it helpful to put a tick next to these. Check the meanings of unfamiliar words (use the glossary at the end of this book or refer to a dictionary or the internet). When practising Section A questions, refer frequently to these two pages so that you get used to using the terms.

## MELODY AND RHYTHM

- Repetition, sequence, imitation
- Ostinato
- Motif
- Inversion, retrograde
- Augmentation, diminution
- Ornamentation (trill, mordent, acciaccatura, etc.)
- Countermelody, descant, obbligato
- Syllabic, melismatic
- Range, tessitura
- Anacrusis
- Hemiola
- Syncopation
- Cross-rhythm, polyrhythm.

## ARTICULATION AND PERFORMANCE

- Staccato, legato
- Sforzando, accent
- Pizzicato, arco, glissando, tremolo
- Sotto voce
- Virtuosic
- Vibrato
- Rubato
- A cappella
- Sprechstimme.

## HARMONY

- Diatonic
- Chromatic
- Dissonant
- Atonal

- Bitonal
- Primary chords, secondary chords, chromatic chords
- Cadences
- Modulation
- Modes (especially dorian, aeolian and myxolydian)
- Harmonic rhythm
- Pedal
- False relation
- Tierce de Picardie
- Tritone.

## TEXTURE

- Monophonic, unison, octaves
- Parallel motion, contrary motion
- Homophonic, chordal
- Polyphonic, contrapuntal
- Block chords, arpeggio, broken chords, triadic
- Antiphony, call and response
- Heterophonic.

## STRUCTURE

- Strophic, through-composed
- Canonic, fugal, stretto
- Verse and chorus.

## TIPS TO IMPROVE YOUR MARK

- Learn the technical vocabulary thoroughly and practise applying it.
- Correct use of a musical term will demonstrate your understanding much more effectively than a whole phrase of vague explanation.
- When asked about choral textures make sure you listen attentively and check carefully with the score whether the singers are singing in unison or in a homophonic texture.
- Be precise about bar numbers: 'It's homophonic' will not gain a mark if the first three bars are in unison and only the fourth bar moves to a chordal texture.
- Do not try to answer questions just by studying the score. Always listen carefully to the relevant bars, consider your response, and only then write your answer.

# Accompaniment

All the music used for Section A in the examination will be accompanied. The accompaniment might be just one instrument (perhaps piano or harp), or full orchestra, or any other instrumental combination. How the composer has employed the instrumental forces will be an important feature of what you are asked. Questions will focus on aspects such as:

- How the introduction sets the scene or mood
- How the accompaniment enhances the text of a particular passage
- The relationship between the vocal part and the accompaniment
- Specific use of instrumental tone colour.

Many of the terms mentioned in 'Musical features' above will be appropriate for use when discussing the accompaniment, and you should also consider the following points:

| Doubling | Does the accompaniment double the voice? <br> If so, is it all the time, or only for particular phrases of text? <br> Does it double at the octave or in unison with the voice? <br> Which instrument doubles the voice? |
| --- | --- |
| Word painting | Are there any words or phrases in the text which are individually enhanced by the instrumental accompaniment? <br> How? |
| Texture | Does this change during the music? <br> Why? <br> Is the vocal line always at the top of the texture with the accompaniment below it? <br> Do the instrumental lines weave in and out of the vocal part? <br> Why? |
| Melody | Are there moments or phrases where the instrumental part takes over the melody, or is the melody always in the voice? <br> Which instrument(s) have the melody? <br> Do any instruments imitate the vocal melody? <br> Does the melody move into a lower part? (The melody is often missed by candidates when it moves into the lowest stave on the score. If you listen you will hear the melodic line even if it is played by one of the lower instruments.) |
| Instrumental tone colour | Does the composer use different instruments for different sections of the text? <br> How does this enhance the text? <br> Are any special techniques such as pizzicato or mutes used? <br> What articulation is used? <br> Remember that the tone colour might change even if there is only one accompanying instrument. |

## TIPS TO IMPROVE YOUR MARK

- Check carefully whether the question is asking about the vocal line, the accompaniment, or both.
- *Listen* to the music with great attention to detail. There might be instrumental parts that have been left out of the music printed in the insert. Make sure you discuss these too where relevant.
- Be as precise as you can. For example:
  'Percussion is added to make it more exciting' is too vague.
  'The tambourine is played on every beat of bar 33, adding to the climax of the phrase' is much more precise and shows you have heard exactly what is happening in the music.

## EXERCISE

Listen to the opening sections of some of the pieces you have studied for Section A and write a short paragraph about the contribution of the accompaniment.

## Harmony and tonality

Remember that *tonality* is one of the Areas of Study for your A2 Music course, so this is an important area. You will be asked specific questions about the harmony and tonality of passages from the extract and will also need to refer to harmony and tonality in more open questions.

Many students find tackling this aspect of the music quite challenging, but if you are methodical in your approach you should improve your understanding and your mark.

It is vital that you know the basics thoroughly: key signatures, key relationships such as relative major/minor, dominant, subdominant. Learn the **circle of 5ths**.

Music from the period 1900–1945 will almost always go beyond these simple relationships, so you need to be prepared to do some detective work:

■ Do not confuse **atonal/atonality** with **chromatic/chromaticism**. In the examination candidates often describe passages from the extract as *atonal* when the music actually uses *chromatic* harmony within a tonal setting.

■ Identify the tonality at the landmarks in the music – the starts of phrases and the cadences.

■ The music in between might be tonally ambiguous, or might modulate rapidly.

■ Look out for progressions of chords where there are added notes – the basic progression might be quite straightforward.

■ The music might include enharmonic change where the chords suddenly go from having lots of flats to lots of sharps or vice versa – for example from F♯ to G♭.

■ The music used in the examination might have **modal** tendencies. You are most likely to encounter music based on the dorian, aeolian and myxolydian modes.

■ Sections of the music might be based on scales such as **pentatonic** or **whole tone**.

## TIPS TO IMPROVE YOUR MARK

■ Know the basics.

■ Don't panic. Even if the passage seems really complicated, there are probably some points where the tonality is clear and the harmony straightforward.

■ Consider the whole passage that is referred to in the question. There might be some ambiguous harmony at the start, but really clear phrases further on where you can pick up marks even if this aspect is not one of your strengths.

■ *Listen* really carefully, sometimes without looking at the score. You should easily detect whether a passage is predominantly major, minor or modal by listening.

■ The composer's choice of tonality and harmony is usually closely linked with how it expresses the text, so always have the meaning of the text in mind.

■ If the question asks about the harmony and tonality of a passage you will not gain marks for writing about how the addition of cymbals and triangle contributes to the excitement (or whatever), so keep your answer relevant to the question.

- Give bar (and beat) numbers to explain your answer more clearly.
- Check through what you have written. It is surprising the number of students who forget to put the flat or sharp signs in when discussing keys and chords. The examiner can only mark what you have written, so if you write about F major even though there are many sharps in the music and you really mean F♯ major, you will not get the mark.
- Try to give some response, even if you are not confident of the answer. Blank spaces do not gain marks!

## EXERCISE

Use every opportunity to improve your understanding of tonality. This does not have to be through study of music specifically for Section A, but might be through careful scrutiny of a passage from a piece you are performing at the moment. For example: in the first section, is the tonality major/minor/modal? In what key does it begin? Does the passage modulate? What chords/cadences are used? Does the music return later in the piece? If so, how is the harmony and tonality different in this second passage?

# Interpretation

Remember that *interpretation* is one of the Areas of Study, so this is another important aspect. You will be asked about how the composer has interpreted the text and may also be asked about the interpretation of the performers on the recording used in the examination.

## HOW THE COMPOSER INTERPRETS THE TEXT

The block of text at the start of Section A on the question paper will be useful here. Re-read the relevant section of text before you attempt the question so that you are sure you know what it is about. The composer might employ any of the features discussed above, and it is up to you to explain your understanding of the interpretation to the examiner.

The question might be about the interpretation of a particular passage in general, or might focus on a particular aspect such as:

- How the introduction sets the scene or mood
- How the accompaniment enhances the setting of the text
- Word painting
- Features of the word setting in the vocal part(s).

## INTERPRETATION BY THE PERFORMERS

Questions on interpretation by the performers require you to demonstrate that you understand how the performers have added their own interpretation to the music. You should listen for aspects of the recording which are not printed in the score. These might include:

- Tempo changes: faster or slower than indicated, unmarked tempo changes, accelerando, ritardando, pause (on a note or a rest), rubato
- Changes in dynamics
- Rhythmic or pitch changes

- Addition of accents, staccato and so on
- Particular emphasis on certain words through extra clear enunciation, rolled 'r' and so on
- Use of sotto voce, vibrato.

## TIPS TO IMPROVE YOUR MARK

- Read the question carefully to find out whether it is asking about how the music interprets the text or how the performers have added their own interpretation.
- Read the relevant section of the text so you have a good feel for what is intended.
- Choose examples to use in your answer before you start writing.
- If the question asks for identification and explanation of *three* examples of word painting, only the first three examples you choose will be marked.
- Identify your examples precisely – use bar/beat numbers and/or the text.
- You must say *why* a point you make is relevant. For example:

'It gets faster in bar 19' only says *what* happens, not *how* this interprets the mood or the text.

'The accelerando in bar 19 reflects the urgency of the text as the boy attempts to run away' says what happens, but also how this is relevant.

## EXERCISE

Listen, with the score, to three vocal pieces from the period 1900–1945 that you have studied and find:

(a) instances where the composer's interpretation is particularly effective

(b) instances where the performers have enhanced the music with their own interpretation.

Then write short notes to describe your findings.

# Comparison question

The final question in Section A requires you to write about another piece of accompanied vocal music from the period 1900–1945 and to compare it with the extract heard in the examination. This question is usually worth 5 marks, and although this might not seem a large proportion of the marks, this is the one part of Section A that you can prepare fully in advance and the marks gained here can make all the difference to your overall score. Study carefully the following paragraphs and the *Tips to improve your mark* and then complete the exercise on page 24 in detail.

As with the whole paper, you should read the question carefully to ensure that the music you choose for comparison is appropriate. The given period will always be 1900–1945, but other aspects will vary from paper to paper.

You might be asked to compare:

- Stylistic features
- Harmony and tonality

- Use of choir and orchestra
- Relationship between voice(s) and accompaniment.

The type of vocal piece might also be stated in the question. You might be asked to select:

- A vocal piece
- A song
- A song with piano accompaniment
- A choral work
- A work for choir and soloist(s)
- A work with orchestral accompaniment
- A stage work
- A setting of text in the English language.

## NOTE

Typical questions would be:

Compare the stylistic features of this extract with those found in another song written between 1900 and 1945 with which you are familiar.

Or:

Compare the use of choir and orchestra in this extract with that found in another choral work from the period 1900–1945.

## TIPS TO IMPROVE YOUR MARK

- Make sure you understand the terminology used in the question. If the question refers to a *vocal* piece, there is no restriction on the music you choose as *vocal* just implies *voice(s)*. If the term *song* is used you should write about a solo song, though it could be a song from a larger work. The term *choral* requires you to write about a work with choir.
- If you choose a large work for discussion, make sure that the section you write about is appropriate to the question. For example, if the question asks you to select a choral work, you should write about a choral movement and not about a solo or duet.
- Identify the piece you choose by title and composer. If you choose something from a larger work name the song or movement as well. For example:

  In Warlock's 'Sleep'…

  In 'By the waters of Babylon' from 'Belshazzar's Feast' by Walton…

- Be accurate in your identification. If the examiner cannot identify the piece you are writing about, you will not gain any marks.
- Keep your answer brief and to the point – note form is fine – and make sure you compare your chosen piece with the examination extract.
- You should be able to discuss precise moments from both pieces to illustrate your answer.
- Revise enough examples from the music you have studied to ensure you are able to select an appropriate piece for comparison in the examination.
- Listen to some of the music from the **suggested further listening** below and make brief notes on a section from each piece.

## EXERCISE

Choose some of the music you have studied for Section A and write separate short paragraphs on each of the following musical aspects:

- Stylistic features such as melody, rhythm, texture and structure
- The accompaniment and its relationship to the voice(s)
- Harmony and tonality.

## SUGGESTED FURTHER LISTENING FOR SECTION A

All the following examples are readily available, e.g. on YouTube.

| Composer | Title | Forces |
|----------|-------|--------|
| Parry | 'I Was Glad' | Choir and orchestra |
| Orff | Carmina Burana | Soloists, choir and orchestra |
| Walton | Belshazzar's Feast | Soloists, choir and orchestra |
| Britten | A Ceremony of Carols | Treble choir and harp – some solo movements |
| Ravel | Trois Poèmes de Stéphane Mallarmé | Voice and instrumental ensemble |
| Schönberg | Pierrot Lunaire | Voice in **Sprechstimme** and instrumental ensemble |
| Vaughan Williams | 'The Vagabond' | Voice and piano |
| Butterworth | A Shropshire Lad | Voice and piano |
| Gershwin | 'Summertime' from Porgy and Bess | Voice and orchestra/piano |

Your school or college may also have past papers from this specification, which will be useful in your preparation.

## NOTE

The music in the *OCR A2 Listening Tests* by Veronica Jamset (Rhinegold Education) will provide further examples from which to choose, as will the suggestions in the *OCR A2 Music Study Guide* by Huw Ellis-Williams and Gavin Richards (Rhinegold Education).

# Practice questions

The following two sample extracts of music are similar to those that might be used for Section A. In the examination the extract will be longer and there will be more questions (totalling 40 marks instead of the 25 here), but these examples show you how to study an unfamiliar piece and will give you a good indication of the sort of questions that you will encounter and will give you some tips on how you might approach this section of the paper.

**NOTE**

Extensive practice for Section A of the examination can be found in the *OCR A2 Listening Tests* by Veronica Jamset (Rhinegold Education).

## EXTRACT 1: LOVELIEST OF TREES

Study the printed music on pages 27 and 28. This is the opening of the song 'Loveliest of Trees' by George Butterworth. It is a setting of words from *A Shropshire Lad* by A.E. Housman.

**NOTE**

There are many recordings of this song available. The recording used for the questions here, particularly relevant in Q4, is by Bryn Terfel and Malcolm Martineau and can be found on Bryn Terfel's album 'The Vagabond'. It is also available on Spotify.

First, consider the text. This will be written out on the actual examination paper.

> Loveliest of trees, the cherry now
> Is hung with bloom along the bough,
> And stands about the woodland ride
> Wearing white for Eastertide.
>
> Now, of my three-score years and ten,
> Twenty will not come again,
> And take from seventy springs a score,
> It only leaves me fifty more.

Notice that the words are in two stanzas – this might have some bearing on the way the composer sets the text. Once you have some feeling for the meaning of the words, listen to the music, following the score (which will be printed in the separate insert) carefully. Then look through the questions so that you can establish the sort of information you will need to provide. Remember that, once the writing time has started, you might find it helpful to mark on the insert the bars used for each question.

## Q1 Describe the music of the first three bars and comment on how it sets the scene. (4)

(Five lines would be given for you to write your answer.)

Before looking at the sample answers below, think about what you would write. Now compare the two sample answers:

### ANSWER A

Melody in the right hand and then the bass plays.
Soft.
Uses pedal.

## ANSWER B

> Introduction for piano. Monophonic, falling scalic melody in E major. Begins in same way as opening vocal phrase. Quiet dynamics and espressivo marking set scene of gentle springtime. Bar 3 has diminuendo on notes of F♯m⁷ chord (chord II⁷) to link to entry of voice.

Both answers are brief and to the point, but it is not difficult to see the difference between them. The first candidate has merely looked at the page and tried to describe what they *see*. They do not realise that the melody is continuous and it is just that the end has been written in the bass clef for convenience. This is a common error – remember that the melodic material may not necessarily be restricted to the highest part, or to the treble clef. This candidate has completely disregarded the second part of the question. The second answer is written in note form, but is clearly expressed. Remember, there is no need to write in continuous prose in Section A. The candidate's answer demonstrates that they *understand* the music. They have said more than enough to gain full marks.

## Q2 Discuss how Butterworth achieves a change of mood for the final line of the first stanza of the poem (bar 13 to bar 18¹). (5)

(Six lines would be given for you to write your answer.)

Once again, think about your answer before you study those given below.

### ANSWER A

> In this section, it is louder with melisma. The piano has big chords and both parts have accidentals.

This is partly accurate, but not well expressed. There is no melisma (the notes are held (tied) over the barline) and the harmonic function of the A♯ is not understood.

### ANSWER B

> In the bars from 13 to 18 the vocal part becomes more emphatic with a crescendo to forte and longer note values. The piano part builds up too and moves through the dominant of the dominant to a clear perfect cadence in E major at bar 15 to 16. The chords are fuller and the moving parts on the tonic and then I⁷ in bars 16 and 17 are loud and emphasised, linking to the celebration of Easter.

This is detailed, but very wordy. There will not be room to write all this in the space provided.

### EXERCISE

Rewrite answer 2 in note form, showing the important aspects of the response and leaving out the padding.

PREPARING FOR G356 SECTION A: AURAL EXTRACT

## Q3 Discuss the expressive use of harmony and tonality in the second stanza (bar 22 to bar 31). (6)

(Seven lines would be given for you to write your answer.)

**NOTE**

**Remember** that *tonality* is one of the Areas of Study, so there will always be some questions relating to it.

Many candidates find questions which relate to tonality much harder to answer than those which relate to interpretation, so it is important that you adopt an organised approach to this type of question in order to do well. This time, instead of sample answers, here is some guidance that sets out a way of working to achieve a good mark:

Study the text again. What do you notice? Is the mood of the text different from the first stanza? In the text the speaker ponders that time is passing him by, that he has already had twenty of his allotted seventy years ('three-score years and ten') and that he is left with only fifty more springs. Now *listen* to the music. It should be immediately obvious that the setting is in a minor key. You should be able to *hear* an implied perfect cadence in bar 24, followed by an interrupted one in bar 26. The harmony then becomes a little more chromatic. Your knowledge of key signatures and tonal relationships should tell you that C♯ minor is the relative minor of the tonic key of the song (E major). Listening to the first few bars of the second stanza should confirm that this is indeed the key used here. The melody is completely **diatonic** and the first two phrases are punctuated only by the outline of the perfect and interrupted cadences. This simplicity reflects the initial idea of the text. The third and fourth lines are coloured with diminished and other chromatic chords as realisation of time passing dawns in the narrator's mind. The strong A–E chords in bar 30 suggest that the music might modulate to A major here, but the F♯ major chord with added 2nd interrupts this. (You cannot tell from the printed extract, but the song continues into a third verse here.)

**EXERCISE**

Study the detailed explanation above and then write an answer to Question 3, writing in note form as you would in the examination.

## Q4 Comment on the expressive interpretation of the performers in this recording. Include specific use of rubato in your answer. (5)

(Six lines would be given for you to write your answer.)

It is very important to realise that this question is asking about the *performance*, not about what the composer has written in the score. Many candidates lose marks on this type of question because they merely repeat what they see in the score: for example, 'There is a crescendo in bar 13.'

The question asks about *expressive* interpretation, so you will not gain marks for saying it is softer or louder (or whatever) without giving an indication of how this interprets the text or mood. The following answer comments on aspects appropriate to the recording identified on page 25.

# ANSWER

♭ 4 voice extends first note of love for emphasis on the word
♭ 19 unmarked rit in the piano prepares for a return to a more reflective mood
♭ 20 much quieter than indicated, to link to...
♭♭ 22–26 sotto voce in voice, almost whispered – undertone suggests personal thoughts
♭♭ 27–29 accelerando emphasises apparent urgency of situation

## EXERCISE

Listen to one or more different recordings of 'Loveliest of Trees' and compare the interpretation with this one. There are several good performances available on YouTube.

## Q5 Compare the tonality of this extract with that found in another accompanied solo song written between 1900 and 1945 with which you are familiar. (5)

(Six lines would be given for you to write your answer.)

The final question in Section A will always require knowledge of another piece of vocal repertoire from this period.

## MARK SCHEME

The examiner will read your answer and place it in the appropriate part of a mark scheme similar to this one when awarding your mark.

| 5 marks | Answers identify strong similarities and/or differences between the tonality of the extract and the chosen song. A number of valid points are made. |
|---------|------------------------------------------------------------------------------------------------------------------------|
| 3–4 marks | Answers identify similarities and/or differences between the tonality of the extract and the chosen song. A few good points are made. |
| 1–2 marks | Answers may show some knowledge but fail to compare successfully the extract with the chosen song; a rather irrelevant answer perhaps referring only partially to tonality. |
| 0 marks | No creditable comparison made, or tonality discussed. |

Study the question carefully and then consider the sample answers given below. Mark them for yourself and then check your marking against the examiner's comments and marks which follow.

## ANSWER A

'Love Bade Me Welcome' by Vaughan Williams is modal. The piano plays mostly quavers, whereas in this extract the piano part sometimes has the melody. There is a more animated section in Vaughan Williams and this extract is more declamatory for Eastertide.

# ANSWER B

Tavener's 'The Lamb' has a tonal centre of G, whereas this piece is in E. 'The Lamb' has a restricted range in the melody and is more chromatic than this piece. The melody keeps returning to G. In this piece, the second verse is in the relative minor.

## ANSWER C

'West London' by Charles Ives begins in D minor, but with a clashing C♯ in the melody to show the plight of the crouching tramp. This extract begins in E major, but the second verse is in the relative minor to depict the thoughts of the narrator. This piece is much more diatonic than 'West London', which has a very chromatic section when the tramp rises above her situation, though the last vocal section is in F major and is completely diatonic, similar to bars 16–19 in this extract.

## EXAMINER'S COMMENTS AND MARKS

### ANSWER A

The music chosen for comparison is appropriate – it is a movement from *Five Mystical Songs*. Always discuss an individual song or movement if you choose a song cycle or something which is divided into movements, rather than generalising about the whole work. Unfortunately, the candidate has not compared the tonality of the two pieces and only says the Vaughan Williams is modal, so would gain only 1 mark.

### ANSWER B

Tavener's 'The Lamb' was written in 1982, so is out of period. It is also a four-part a cappella choral work, so would be an inappropriate choice for comparison for this reason too. No marks would be awarded.

### ANSWER C

This answer gives a number of specific details about the extract and the chosen song. The candidate demonstrates that they know the music and can select appropriate examples for illustration. This answer would gain 5 marks.

## EXTRACT 2: A SEA SYMPHONY

Study the printed music on pages 32–36. The music is from 'Scherzo – The Waves' from *A Sea Symphony* by Vaughan Williams. The words are by Walt Whitman.

### NOTE

There are a number of recordings of this work available. Any recording would be suitable for you to use to answer the questions.

First, consider the text:

> *After the sea-ship, after the whistling winds,*
> *After the white-gray sails taut to their spars and ropes,*
> *Below, a myriad, myriad waves hastening, lifting up their necks,*

Listen to the music, following the score carefully. Notice that as the male voices do not enter at the start their parts are omitted until they begin. Then look through the questions and listen to the extract for a second time.

## Q1  Describe the choral textures. (5)

(Six lines would be given for you to write your answer.)

Before looking at the sample answers below, think about what you would write. Now compare the three sample answers and examiner's comments:

## ANSWER A

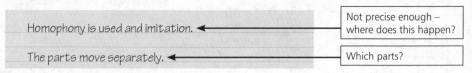

Homophony is used and imitation. ← Not precise enough – where does this happen?

The parts move separately. ← Which parts?

## ANSWER B

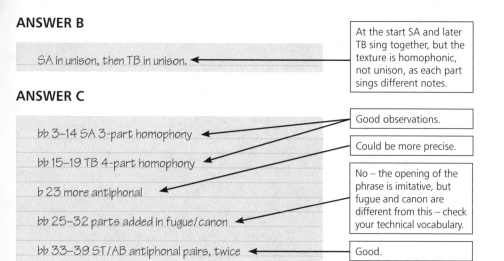

SA in unison, then TB in unison. ◄━━━ At the start SA and later TB sing together, but the texture is homophonic, not unison, as each part sings different notes.

## ANSWER C

bb 3–14 SA 3-part homophony ◄━━━ Good observations.

bb 15–19 TB 4-part homophony ◄━━━ Could be more precise.

b 23 more antiphonal ◄━━━ No – the opening of the phrase is imitative, but fugue and canon are different from this – check your technical vocabulary.

bb 25–32 parts added in fugue/canon ◄━━━

bb 33–39 ST/AB antiphonal pairs, twice ◄━━━ Good.

Answer A would not gain any marks, because the candidate has just named some textures without reference to the music.

Answer B only refers to vocal forces, so would not gain any marks either. Misinterpretation of *unison* when the parts are only rhythmically the same is a common error, so take care!

Answer C would score 4 marks. Bar numbers are indicated to pinpoint answers. It is fine to abbreviate SATB for soprano, alto and so on as long as what you write is clear. The candidate has clearly noticed the change of texture at bars 25–32, but has chosen the wrong term to describe it, so this cannot be credited.

## Q2   Discuss the tonality and harmony of the passage from bar 1 to bar 25[1]. (5)

(Six lines would be given for you to write your answer.)

Once again, think about your answer before you study those given below.

## ANSWER A

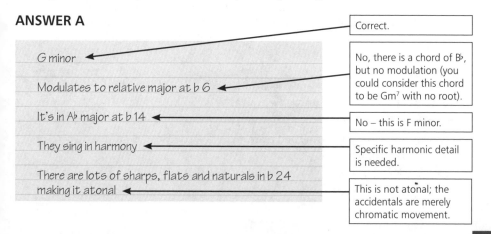

G minor ◄━━━ Correct.

Modulates to relative major at b 6 ◄━━━ No, there is a chord of B♭, but no modulation (you could consider this chord to be Gm[7] with no root).

It's in A♭ major at b 14 ◄━━━ No – this is F minor.

They sing in harmony ◄━━━ Specific harmonic detail is needed.

There are lots of sharps, flats and naturals in b 24 making it atonal ◄━━━ This is not atonal; the accidentals are merely chromatic movement.

## ANSWER B

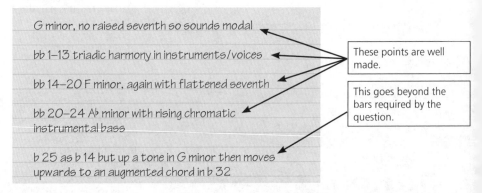

G minor, no raised seventh so sounds modal

bb 1–13 triadic harmony in instruments/voices

bb 14–20 F minor, again with flattened seventh

bb 20–24 A♭ minor with rising chromatic instrumental bass

b 25 as b 14 but up a tone in G minor then moves upwards to an augmented chord in b 32

> These points are well made.

> This goes beyond the bars required by the question.

Answer A would score only 1 mark. The answer is confused and does not demonstrate understanding of technical vocabulary related to tonality.

Answer B would gain full marks, but the candidate wastes valuable time discussing bars which are outside those demanded by the question. This is a common error, so be careful!

### EXERCISE

Consider the harmony and tonality of the remainder of the extract from bar 25 to bar 39. Use the superfluous response at the end of Answer B as a starting point.

### Q3 Discuss ways in which the music enhances the text in the extract. Refer to aspects of rhythm, word painting and orchestration in your answer. (10)

(Twelve lines would be given for you to write your answer.)

This question, which requires a more extended answer, would probably have a holistic mark scheme as described on page 16. Consider the question carefully and then listen to the music, following the score. Mark on the score anything you notice as you go along, then decide what to write and in what order. Make sure you have included reference to all the aspects addressed in the question. You do not need to address each aspect separately – a comment on one bar or passage might refer to rhythm, word painting and orchestration.

### NOTE

**Remember** you must give detailed examples to do well.

The examiner will read your answer and place it in the appropriate part of the mark scheme when awarding your mark.

Answers might include:

- Opening brass G minor chords are like a call to order; the two quavers (also played by *pizz* strings) and the silence which follows are expectant after the held note; sets the scene.
- Closely placed triads in SSA with triplet rhythms are fanfare-like.
- Syllabic setting (lightly doubled by the woodwind and horns) helps clarity of text.
- Rising violin arpeggio and high tremolo from b8 suggest whistling wind.
- Off-beat entry of the woodwind/brass in b9³ gives a syncopated effect.
- From b14 swirling octave strings, again using triplets, suggests the waves of the text.
- b15³ the trombones begin very low in range for 'below', and phrase then rises and falls like the waves with horns joining the vocal parts homophonically.
- Addition of timpani and occasional cymbal crash adds to low rumbling effect of waves.
- From b20² opening text repeated for emphasis; this time with string tremolo rising chromatic scale starting in low tessitura adding to *brillante* marking.
- b24 rising quadruplet chromatic movement in SSA and high woodwind imitates whistling of winds.
- Insistent triplets in bb33/36 moves the music on, as does rising chromatic scale in bb37–38.

## Q4 Compare the stylistic features of this extract with those found in another choral work written between 1900 and 1945 with which you are familiar. (5)

(Six lines would be given for you to write your answer.)

### MARK SCHEME

| 5 marks | Answers identify strong similarities and/or differences between the stylistic features of the extract and the chosen work. A number of valid points are made. |
|---|---|
| 3–4 marks | Answers identify similarities and/or differences between the stylistic features of the extract and the chosen work. A few good points are made. |
| 1–2 marks | Answers may show some knowledge but fail to compare successfully the extract with the chosen work. |
| 0 marks | No creditable comparison made. |

Study the question carefully and then consider the sample answers given below. Mark them for yourself and then check your marking against the examiner's comments and marks which follow.

### ANSWER A

The style seems to change during the piece with the brass and strings and voices. In Stravinsky's Oedipus Rex there is an operatic voice and a choir in the background, whereas this piece has no soloist.

## ANSWER B

Rio Grande is a choral piece written by Constant Lambert. It is similar in style to this piece, using the orchestra and choir to good effect. It starts in a major key, but is highly chromatic.

## ANSWER C

'Loveliest of Trees' is similar to this piece. They are both written in English. 'Loveliest of Trees' begins in the major, whereas this begins in the minor. This has full orchestra, not just piano.

## EXAMINER'S COMMENTS AND MARKS

### ANSWER A

This is very generalised with no detail. The candidate has clearly listened to just one section of *Oedipus Rex* where there is a solo with accompanying chorus, but writes as though this is all that happens in the work. (1 mark)

### ANSWER B

This has some relevant points, but lacks detail and does not compare successfully. (2 marks)

### ANSWER C

The composer of the chosen piece is not identified. The candidate is probably referring to Butterworth (used for Sample Extract 1) as extracts used in previous papers are often cited. However, the candidate has confused 'vocal' and 'choral': 'Loveliest of Trees' is a solo song, not a choral work, so this is not an appropriate choice for comparison. (0 marks)

### EXERCISE

Revise items of vocal music written in the period 1900–1945 that you have studied and then write appropriate answers for Extract 1 Question 5 and Extract 2 Question 4.

# Preparing for G356 Section B: Historical Topics

## What is required

In Section B you are required to write **two** essays. Three questions will be provided on each of the six historical topics and you may answer any two questions. Centres usually prepare their students for only one topic (though you might have covered more than one), so you should obviously choose from the questions on the topic(s) you have studied.

## TOP TIPS

- Write your essays in the answer booklet.
- Make sure you identify which questions you attempt.
- Write legibly. If the examiner cannot decipher what you have written you will not gain the marks. Many students find it hard to write clearly at speed. Practise this regularly, perhaps by hand-writing all your preparatory essays. This will help you in all your subjects, not just music.
- You will need to demonstrate detailed knowledge and understanding of the music and will have to write in clear English with correct spelling, punctuation and grammar, using appropriate musical terminology, in order to gain a high mark.
- The inclusion of musical quotations on manuscript paper is a useful way of showing the examiner that you know the precise detail of the music you are discussing. However, there is no point writing out a whole list of quotes which you do not refer to in your essay. Any quotes should be brief and accurate. Remember to include the correct clef and key signature. Cross reference the quote in your essay. For example:

  …in the *pp* monophonic opening of the main theme played on the flute and violin (quote 1),…

## How to prepare for Section B

- Study this section of the book (pages 41 to 53) carefully, considering, as you read, how the information relates to the topic you are revising.
- The next section (pages 53–55) gives useful tips for revision and is followed by some sample essays covering each topic. This will help you when you revise your notes and write practice essays.

## Historical topics

For each topic there are three items of prescribed repertoire which you must know in detail. You do not have to learn the whole of each of the works, but should learn enough movements/numbers/extended passages to be able to demonstrate that you have a thorough understanding of the musical features of the piece. You will also study related repertoire, which will help you put the prescribed repertoire into the context of other music that was being composed at the same time.

Remember that questions will be linked to the Areas of Study – tonality and interpretation – so you will need to show that you have in-depth knowledge of these areas in relation to the music you have studied.

The following table lists the historical topics together with the associated prescribed and related repertoire. Check which topic(s) you are studying. The topics will appear in this order on the examination paper.

| | Prescribed repertoire | Related repertoire |
|---|---|---|
| **Topic 1:** **Song** | Dowland, *The First Booke of Songes* | English and Italian madrigals, music for solo lute, English consort music |
| | Schumann, *Dichterliebe* | Early 19th-century lieder, early Romantic character pieces for piano |
| | Maxwell Davies, *Eight Songs for a Mad King* | Solo songs with piano/instrumental combinations since 1950 |
| **Topic 2:** **Programme music** | Vivaldi, *The Four Seasons* | Early 18th-century programme music (e.g. French keyboard music, Italian instrumental music) |
| | Berlioz, *Symphonie fantastique* | 19th-century symphonic poems and programmatic overtures |
| | MacMillan, *The Confession of Isobel Gowdie* | Descriptive instrumental music since 1950 |
| **Topic 3:** **Music for the screen** | Korngold, *The Adventures of Robin Hood* | Early film scores by mainstream composers in the post-Mahlerian tradition |
| | Herrmann, *Vertigo* | Film scores that explore increasing integration between music and dramatic action |
| | Glass, *The Hours* | Film scores that use modern adaptations of composing techniques (e.g. leitmotif, minimalist procedures) |
| **Topic 4:** **Music and belief** | Byrd, *Mass for Four Voices* | English motets and anthems from the late 16th and early 17th centuries |
| | Bach, *St Matthew Passion* | Handel oratorio, smaller-scale Baroque works (e.g. cantata, ode) for voices and instrumental combinations |
| | Stockhausen, *Stimmung* | Works since 1950 which demonstrate the influence(s) of beliefs and/or religious traditions (e.g. Eastern, Orthodox, African, Buddhist) |
| **Topic 5:** **Music for the stage** | Purcell, *Dido and Aeneas* | Court masque and theatre music in England |
| | Wagner, *Die Walküre* | A contemporary Italian opera |
| | Bernstein, *West Side Story* | Contrasting examples of stage musicals and/or operas since 1945 |

| Topic 6:<br>Popular music | The Beatles, *Sgt Pepper's Lonely Hearts Club Band* | British pop music (groups and solo artists) from the 1960s |
|---|---|---|
| | Queen, *A Night at the Opera* | Examples of 1970s glam rock, music by 'super groups' with international fame |
| | Norah Jones, *Not Too Late* | Examples of music from contemporary singer/songwriters |

# Managing your time effectively

- You will have about one hour to write the two essays in Section B. This is not much time and it will need to be used wisely. There are 25 marks for each essay. You should aim to complete them both as well as you are able. If you do not allow enough time for your second essay, you will be throwing marks away.
- Look at the essay titles for the topic(s) you have studied. Decide which questions suit you best. Think about:
  - Which questions give you an opportunity to write about the music you are most comfortable with?
  - Have you read the question properly? How many works does it require you to discuss?
- Once you have chosen your questions, write a brief plan. You can use a page of the answer booklet for this. Label it 'plan' and leave a gap before you start your essay so that the examiner knows where your answer begins. Remember to write the question number in the margin.
- Write your first essay using your plan to help you – there are tips on this later in this chapter.
- Keep an eye on the time. You should have about 30 minutes for each essay.
- Leave a gap before you plan your second essay. It is a good idea to start on a new page of the answer booklet, and then if you decide to add anything to the first essay there should be enough space to do so.
- Try to leave time to check through your work.

## NOTE

Make sure during your revision sessions you practise writing essays to a time limit. Then you will be better prepared for the time constraints of the actual examination.

# The layout of the questions

As has already been noted, there will be three questions on each topic. The layout of the questions is similar for each topic on every examination paper.

| First question | This will address aspects of **one** of the **prescribed works** for the topic. |
|---|---|
| Second question | This will be a comparison or discussion of: |
| | ■ *either* **two** of the **prescribed works** |
| | ■ *or* **one prescribed work** and some **related repertoire**. |

| Third question | This might relate to **any aspect of the topic**, and you should be prepared to draw on the prescribed and related repertoire as well as knowledge of the social or cultural conditions influencing the work of composers during the time covered by the topic. |
|---|---|

As you can see, if you are studying just one topic, you will need to cover all three prescribed works and some related repertoire in order to be able to answer two questions in the examination.

## Different types of question

Within the basic layout of the questions given above, the actual questions will take various formats.

Questions will begin in different ways:

- Discuss...
- Illustrate...
- Comment on...
- Explain...
- Compare...
- Give a detailed account of...

What follows will depend partly on the topic, but might be:

- ...the expressive use of timbre and texture in...
- ...the expressive use of harmony and tonality in...
- ...the harmonic and tonal processes in...
- ...the expressive use of melody and structure in...
- ...the effectiveness of the descriptive writing in...
- ...the effectiveness of the word setting in...
- ...the musical interpretation of lyrics and/or mood in...
- ...the expressive instrumental techniques in...
- ...the vocal techniques in...
- ...the role of the chorus in...
- ...the integration of voice(s) and accompaniment in...
- ...the ways in which the drama is interpreted in...
- ...the relationship between music and dramatic action in...
- ...the musical techniques used in the interpretation of dialogue and action in...
- ...the relationship between voice and instruments in ...
- ...the musical characteristics of...
- ...the expressive characteristics of...
- ...the interpretation of subject matter in...
- ...the transformation of themes in...
- ...the use of leitmotifs in...
- ...the use of technology and recording processes in...

Depending on whether it is the first, second or third question on the topic, the question will end with the title(s), composer(s) or time period of the music to be discussed. For example:

First question

- …Schumann's *Dichterliebe*.
- …*The Confession of Isobel Gowdie*.
- …Korngold's music for *The Adventures of Robin Hood*.
- …Stockhausen's *Stimmung*.
- …*West Side Story*.
- …*A Night at the Opera*.

Second question

- …the songs of Maxwell Davies and one other composer writing since 1950.
- …the songs of Dowland and Schumann.
- …*Symphonie fantastique* and another programmatic work of the 19th century.
- …*The Four Seasons* and *Symphonie fantastique*.
- …the film music of Glass and one other contemporary composer.
- …the film music of Korngold and Herrmann.
- …the religious music of Bach and Handel.
- …Byrd's *Mass for Four Voices* and Bach's *St Matthew Passion*.
- …*Dido and Aeneas* and another work for the English stage from the same period.
- …music for the stage by Wagner and Bernstein.
- …the songs of The Beatles and another British group of the 1960s.
- …the songs of Queen and Norah Jones.

Third question

- …the music of two composers of Lieder writing in the early 19th century.
- …music for the lute as solo and accompanying instrument in Dowland's time.
- …two post-1950 descriptive instrumental works by different composers.
- …the descriptive instrumental music of two composers of the Baroque period.
- …two recent film scores by different composers.
- …two film scores by composers writing in the post-Mahlerian tradition.
- …English motets and anthems of the late 16th and early 17th century.
- …two musical interpretations of belief by different composers writing since 1950.
- …any two works for the stage by different composers writing since 1945.
- …two 19th-century stage works, putting them into their cultural and social context.
- …the music of at least two contemporary singer-songwriters.
- …the music of two glam rock bands of the 1970s.

Especially in the first question for each topic, there will often be an indication of the minimum amount of the music that you should discuss in your answer. For example:

- Refer in detail to at least four songs.
- Give examples from at least two movements.
- Refer in detail to at least three scenes.
- Discuss at least two extended passages.
- Discuss at least four tracks.

Putting together these beginnings, middles and ends will create whole questions similar to those found in the examination. For example:

- Discuss the expressive use of timbre and texture in *The Confession of Isobel Gowdie*. Refer in detail to at least two extended passages.
- Compare the relationship between music and dramatic action in the film music of Korngold and Herrmann.
- Give a detailed account of the interpretation of subject matter in two 19th-century stage works, putting them into their cultural and social context.

## EXERCISE

Produce essay titles of your own from the beginnings, middles and ends given above. Create two for each of the first, second and third question on the topic you are studying. Choose phrases which are appropriate to the topic – you might need to change the wording slightly to make the essay titles make sense. Refer to the table of historical topics on page 42 if you need some help with the related repertoire. Keep your titles safe, so that you can write the essays later when you have read the rest of this chapter. If you work diligently through every appropriate combination of phrases from those given above (inserting works from the prescribed and related repertoire for your selected topic), you will have covered a good range of essays in preparation for the examination.

## NOTE

If you work diligently through every appropriate combination of phrases from those given above (inserting works from the prescribed and related repertoire for your selected topic), you will have covered the essence of almost every question likely to appear in the examination.

## The mark scheme

It is important that you have an understanding of the mark scheme used by examiners so that you know how to get a good mark. The table below is like the one used to assess all essays in Section B. The examiner will decide where your essay best fits in the mark scheme when awarding your mark.

Remember that you are required to demonstrate your understanding of issues relating to the areas of study **tonality** and **interpretation**.

Study the mark scheme thoroughly. You will see that several aspects of your work are assessed:

- How detailed your **knowledge** is
- How well you know **relevant examples** from the music
- How well you understand the **context**
- How well you answer the **specific question**
- How well you express yourself in **written English**.

| Mark | Categorised by |
|------|----------------|
| 22–25 | Thorough and detailed knowledge of the appropriate aspect of the chosen topic, supported by close familiarity with a wide range of relevant examples of music and an extensive understanding of context, with a clear demonstration of the ability to apply this knowledge and understanding to answering the specific question. Answers clearly expressed in language of high quality, essentially without faults of grammar, punctuation and spelling. |
| 18–21 | Specific knowledge of the appropriate aspect of the chosen topic, supported by close familiarity with a range of relevant examples of music and a good understanding of context, with evidence of the ability to apply this knowledge and understanding to answering the specific question. Answers clearly expressed in language of mainly good quality, with perhaps occasional lapses of grammar, punctuation and spelling. |
| 15–17 | Good knowledge of the appropriate aspect of the chosen topic, supported by some familiarity with a range of relevant examples, not entirely precise in detail and with a general understanding of context, but not always able to apply this knowledge and understanding to answering the specific question. Answers expressed with moderate clarity with some flaws in grammar, punctuation and spelling. |
| 12–14 | Some knowledge of the appropriate aspect of the chosen topic, but relatively superficial, partly supported by familiarity with some relevant examples and some understanding of context, but only partly able to apply this knowledge and understanding to answering the specific question. Answers partially clear in their expression with faults in grammar, punctuation and spelling. |
| 9–11 | Some knowledge of the chosen topic, partly supported by familiarity with some music, but insecure and not always relevant. A general understanding of context not directly applied to answering the specific question. Answers poorly expressed in places with persistent weaknesses in spelling, punctuation and grammar. |
| 6–8 | A little knowledge of the chosen topic with little familiarity with music and sketchy understanding of context. A series of vague and unrelated points not attempting to address the question, and poorly expressed in incorrect language. |
| 0–5 | Barely any knowledge of the chosen topic, music or understanding of context. No attempt to address the question. Very poor quality of language throughout. |

## KNOWLEDGE

This is where you show how well you know the appropriate aspect of the topic you have studied:

- Have you chosen suitable works for discussion?
- Do you know about relevant musical features such as timbre and texture, harmony and tonality, melody and structure?
- Have you used appropriate musical terminology?

## RELEVANT EXAMPLES

This is where your decisions about exactly which sections of the music to discuss are important:

- Have you chosen suitable passages?
- Have you written about them in detail?
- Are you able to quote a short extract if relevant?

## CONTEXT

This is where you show your understanding of the background of the music you have chosen to discuss:

- Can you place the passage correctly in the whole work?
- Do you know how the work fits in with others written in the same period?
- Do you know whether the musical features you write about are typical of the composer or the period?
- Do you know how any relevant social and cultural issues have influenced the music?

## THE SPECIFIC QUESTION

This is where many candidates lose marks:

- Have you written about the number of works asked for in the question?
- Have you chosen an appropriate number of passages/scenes/movements for discussion?
- Have you confined your writing to the right aspect, for example harmony and tonality?

## WRITTEN ENGLISH

This is where how well you write is assessed:

- Is your spelling correct? Pay particular attention to the composer's name, titles of music, technical terminology.
- Have you used correct punctuation, including appropriate use of capital letters in titles of music?
- Have you set out your work in paragraphs?
- Have you used correct grammar without colloquialisms?

## NOTE

If you know that spelling is not your strongest point, make a list of key words that you often misspell and learn them.

## EXAMPLES OF HOW THE MARK SCHEME IS APPLIED

These three short essay extracts will help you get a better feeling for the mark scheme. Read each question and the answer that follows. The essays might not be on the historical topic that you have studied, but they will still increase your understanding of what is required. Note the observations on the right carefully and then see where you think the essay extract fits in the mark scheme before reading the examiner comments below.

## Question A
## Comment on the musical interpretation of lyrics in the songs of The Beatles and another British group of the 1960s.

This is all the student wrote.

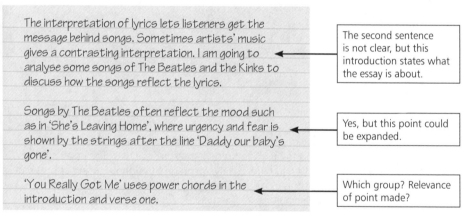

The interpretation of lyrics lets listeners get the message behind songs. Sometimes artists' music gives a contrasting interpretation. I am going to analyse some songs of The Beatles and the Kinks to discuss how the songs reflect the lyrics.

The second sentence is not clear, but this introduction states what the essay is about.

Songs by The Beatles often reflect the mood such as in 'She's Leaving Home', where urgency and fear is shown by the strings after the line 'Daddy our baby's gone'.

Yes, but this point could be expanded.

'You Really Got Me' uses power chords in the introduction and verse one.

Which group? Relevance of point made?

Examiner comments: this is very brief. The comment about 'She's Leaving Home' is relevant, but not detailed enough. The Kinks is an appropriate group for comparison with The Beatles, but the student has not made clear that 'You Really Got Me' is by the Kinks, and the point they have made about the song is not linked to the question. The student has probably run out of time and has not been able to demonstrate their full understanding, although the quality of their written English is reasonable. Little knowledge or familiarity with the music is shown in this very short essay, which would score around 7 out of 25, well below the mark required to pass.

## Question B
## Illustrate the expressive use of harmony and tonality in at least two extended passages from *Die Walküre*.

This is the opening of a much longer essay that continued in a similar way.

Wagner fully utilises the tonal system, stretching its limits in order to express his drama.

> This is a strong opening. It gets straight down to detailed examples from the music.

In Act 1 Scene 3 of Die Walküre, after an A minor and D♯ diminished chord, Wagner begins with Hunding's leitmotif on a C timpani note (♭5) soon moving to A (♭11) and becoming a pedal note under alternating chords of A minor and B⁷. This expresses the tension of the scene and Siegmund's anxious state as he thinks about how he needs his father's sword. This section lacks a clear key, adding to his sense of isolation and abandonment. However, at ♭23, when Siegmund cries 'Ein Schwert', the music is firmly in F minor, expressing his desire to have the sword. When Siegmund's thoughts turn to Sieglinde, the A pedal note becomes the third of an F⁷ chord, which becomes the dominant of B♭ major, as the music becomes much more expressive. The tension is built up using different harmonisations of the A pedal.

Examiner comments: this student is able to show that they have thorough and detailed knowledge and demonstrate close familiarity with the music. They have been precise about chords and keys and where they occur. They have also said how this links to the storyline, thus showing how harmony and tonality are used in an expressive way. The essay answers the specific question and is written in high-quality language throughout, using appropriate musical terminology. Given that this essay opening continued in the same way with a number of detailed examples, it would score full marks.

## Question C
## Explain the effectiveness of the descriptive writing in at least two movements from Vivaldi's *The Four Seasons*.

This is all the student wrote.

I am going to write about how two movements from the first concerto, 'Spring' show the effectiveness of Vivaldis descriptive writting.

The solo violin is used to show the birds in springtime. It plays semiquavers for the cuckoo, a dotted rythm for the turtle dove and high alternating notes for the goldfinch in E major.

> Confused. There are three violins which depict the birds in 'Spring'. The music described here is in the 'Summer' concerto, although the key is correct for 'Spring'.

After the return of the main tune there is a storm. There are quick notes starting on E in the whole orchestra in unison. Then there are quick rising scales.

> The 'main tune' is the ritornello – use the correct musical term. The repeated note is B, not E.

In the second movement, Vivaldi writes about a sleeping goatherd and his dog. There are three main musical ideas. The solo violins long legarto melody in the relative minor represents the sleeping goatherd and the rustling of leaves is shown in the dotted figures played in thirds by the orchestral violins. The viola plays a gruff disjointed quaver crochet rythm which is for the dogs bark. There is no bass line in this movement.

> The comments on the second movement are more accurate, though rather brief.

> The viola forms the bass line.

Examiner comments: this student has become confused about the music in the different concertos that make up *The Four Seasons*. They have referred to the storm, but could have given much more detail about how the music reflects the poetry used by Vivaldi. They know the second movement in more detail, but have not explained the effectiveness of the descriptive writing as required by the question. There are several errors of spelling (*writing*, *rhythm*, *legato* and *crotchet*) and punctuation (apostrophes have been omitted in *Vivaldi's*, *violin's* and *dog's*). This student shows some relatively superficial knowledge and some familiarity with relevant examples from the music, although much of what they say is insecure and they do not really answer the question. The essay would score around 11 or 12 out of 25, a little above the mark required to pass. If the student had learnt the first movement of 'Spring' as well as they knew the second one, they could have improved their mark.

---

**NOTE**

Further sample essays appear at the end of this chapter.

---

# Expectations

- The examination is designed to be completed in the given time (1¾ hours + 15 minutes preparation time), so you should do your very best to answer all the questions in Section A and write two essays for Section B.
- The examiner will expect that you have studied the prescribed repertoire in detail and that you can refer closely to the music in your answers.
- You will be expected to discuss music you have studied for the related repertoire and to make pertinent comparisons with relevant aspects of the prescribed repertoire.
- You should be able to discuss how the composer has used tonality and how the subject matter (text, programme, film, libretto, lyrics) has been interpreted in the music.
- The examiner will expect you to answer the specific question that has been set.
- You are expected to write in continuous prose using sentences and paragraphs.
- You are expected to write legibly using correct English.

# Pitfalls – things to avoid

There are some areas where even students who have revised thoroughly lose marks:

## MISUNDERSTANDING OF CENTURIES

For example, consider the question:

> Discuss how the music interprets the drama in two 19th-century works for the stage.

A student writes about *West Side Story* (1957) and *Jesus Christ Superstar* (1971). They mistakenly thought that 19th century is the same as 1900s. However good the essay, it cannot gain a mark as the chosen repertoire is inappropriate to the question.

## WRITING ABOUT MORE (OR FEWER) WORKS THAN DEMANDED BY THE QUESTION

For example, consider the question:

> Illustrate the effectiveness of the interpretation of lyrics in the music of The Beatles.

A student has revised an essay entitled 'Illustrate the effectiveness of the interpretation of lyrics in the music of The Beatles and Queen'. They write the essay they have prepared. Everything about Queen will be disregarded as it is irrelevant to the question. The student has wasted a lot of examination time and has probably not written enough on the music of The Beatles to gain a high mark.

If you turn this scenario around and the student only writes about The Beatles when they are supposed to write about Queen as well, they cannot gain a high mark as they have only answered half the question.

## DUPLICATING MATERIAL IN THE TWO ESSAYS

There is a reminder regarding this at the start of Section B. You cannot be rewarded twice for making the same point in both essays. It is fine to use the same section of the music if, for example, in the first essay you discuss the expressive harmony and tonality of the passage and in the second essay you write about instrumental techniques, but you must not use exactly the same information, for example making the same points about the role of the accompaniment in a particular passage in both essays.

# How to improve your mark

You will have learned many things about essay writing during your course. The following tips should help you write a successful essay during the examination itself.

- Plan your time in the examination. As soon as the writing time begins, note down what the time will be after 45 minutes (the very latest you should be starting your first essay) and 30 minutes later than that (when you should be starting your second essay). (You might decide a slightly different time schedule suits you better. If so, adapt the timings as necessary.) Try to stick to your time schedule. If you run out of time for Section A, leave it and do the essays. Most students find it easier to pick up marks on the essays as this is the section they have been able to prepare for most fully.

- Read all the questions on your selected topic(s) carefully. Underline the key words in the questions so that you are sure you fully understand their meaning. Then reflect on what music you know in detail which is relevant to each question. It should now be evident which questions you will be able to answer most successfully – don't take too much time deciding, as the minutes will be ticking away.
- Once you have decided which question to answer, plan your essay. This will be time well spent and will enable you to write a well-organised, focused essay more quickly. You might prefer to jot down brief notes as words or phrases, to use bullet points or maybe a spider diagram. Whatever your method, your plan should help you to get started and should enable you to write your essay in a coherent manner which is easy for the examiner to understand.
- Label the plan and leave a space under it before you start the actual essay.
- Your opening paragraph should outline how you intend to answer the question. Do not waffle, but focus on the question itself. There is no need to give extensive background information. You need to state immediately what your approach to the essay will be.
- The body of your essay should be written in clearly organised paragraphs. Try to make one key point, perhaps on one section or aspect of the music you are discussing, and develop it in each paragraph. Make the paragraphs lead on from each other in a logical fashion. Linking words and phrases such as 'Secondly…', 'Another example is…' or 'Conversely…' can be used to help the paragraphs flow well.
- Refer closely to the music in your answer. Be as precise as you can about aspects of the music that answer the specific question. There is no point in just writing everything you know without reference to the question.
- Make sure you include enough detailed examples to fulfil the demands of the question and also to show you know the music well, but it is usually better to write thoroughly about a few sections rather than vaguely about a lot.
- Include brief quotations from the music on manuscript paper only where relevant. For a quote to be worthwhile, it should be accurate and needs to relate directly to a point of discussion in your essay.
- Your closing paragraph needs to round off the essay. You need to summarise what you have said, without merely repeating your earlier content, and, if the question asked you to make some sort of judgement, this is where you should express your opinion and the reasons for it. It is often useful to begin the closing paragraph with a word or phrase such as 'Finally…', 'In conclusion…' or 'As I have shown…' to signal to the reader that you are about to sum up – it also shows the examiner that this is where the essay is really intended to end and it isn't finishing just because you have run out of time!
- If you do find you are short of time, try to write short bullet point notes on any issues you have not been able to discuss in detail. This is better than nothing and the examiner will give you some credit for any relevant points you make, although remember that the expectation is that you will write in full sentences and paragraphs.

## Tips for revision for Section B

When it comes to revision there are many different approaches. Some students like to rewrite their notes, while others make coloured charts of key facts. Some like to work in the morning, others in the evening. Whatever your preference, some aspects are fundamental and are essential to successful revision.

## ORGANISING YOURSELF

- It seems obvious, but it is vital to get organised. Find everything to do with your Section B work. This will include:
  - Class notes
  - Teacher handouts
  - Notes from your own research
  - Scores
  - Audio files (CD/MP3)
  - Study guides.
- The glossary at the back of this revision guide also contains key information.
- Sort out all these materials so that you know what refers to each of the prescribed and related works you have studied. Does anything seem to be missing? Check with your classmates or teacher. Make sure you know how each item of related repertoire relates to the prescribed works.

## PLANNING YOUR TIME

You need to allocate enough time to learn and to revisit your learning.

- Start with your chosen sections from the prescribed works and then take the related repertoire in turn.
- Be realistic about how much you can learn in one session and about how much time overall you have to spend on this subject, given all the other revision you have to do.
- Try to make each session varied by allowing time for reading, making notes, listening to the music and testing yourself.
- As you progress with your revision, write essay plans and timed essays – see tips below.

## MAKING NOTES

- You should condense all the information you have already into notes which are more manageable to revise in the time leading up to the examination. Depending on your learning preferences, you might choose one or more of the following methods:
  - Lists
  - Spider diagrams
  - Bubble charts
  - Prompt cards.
- Make sure you include enough detail to use in your essays, but not so much that you cannot learn it.
- As you progress you might find it helpful to make notes from the notes, so that you just have the key facts to remind you of the detailed information.

## WRITING TIMED ESSAYS

- Get plenty of practice at writing timed essays during your revision sessions. Use the pen you will use in the examination.
- Look back at the examples on pages 44–45 to help you create suitable essay titles.
- Make sure you include all features that might appear in the examination.

- Pay particular attention to including aspects (such as tonality) that you find difficult.
- Mark each essay for yourself by referring to the mark scheme on page 47 and using your notes for specific detail.
- Make a list of things you omitted and rewrite the essay if necessary.

## WRITING ESSAY PLANS

During your revision period, you will not have time to write every possible examination essay title. Good plans can be just as valuable as whole essays for revision purposes.

- Read the question and highlight or underline the key words.
- Make a list of the sections from each work of prescribed and/or related repertoire that would be appropriate for discussion.
- Choose which to use and put them into a logical order for each paragraph.
- Check your selection matches what is required in the question.
- Add some detail to each item of your list so that the plan will be useful for revision.

## CHOOSING PASSAGES OF MUSIC

- You need to revise in depth enough sections of each work you have studied to be able to demonstrate your thorough understanding of tonality and interpretation in relation to those works. It is difficult to be prescriptive about how much to learn, as each work is different and individual students can cope with varying amounts of material. However, it is better to revise a few passages really well than to have only vague knowledge of the whole work.
- Some extended passages (movements/songs/scenes) from the music you have studied as prescribed and related repertoire could be described as 'multipurpose' in the examination situation. That is, you could write about them in relation to tonality, but also in relation to various aspects of interpretation (such as word setting, accompaniment, thematic development or texture). Learning such passages thoroughly will mean you can adapt their use to several different examination questions.

## LEARNING QUOTATIONS FROM THE MUSIC

- Including short, accurate quotes in the examination will show the examiner that you know the detail of the melody, rhythm or chords you are writing about.
- Write out some quotes and put them with your notes. As well as being useful in the examination, this will help you to learn the music during your revision sessions.
- There is no need to learn lots of quotes. Just limit yourself to a few from each work that you can remember well.

## LISTENING TO THE MUSIC

- Last, but certainly not least, you should spend time listening attentively to the music you have studied. The examiner wants to find out how well you know the actual music. Concentrate on getting to know aurally the passages you have chosen to revise in depth, but remember to think about the context of the whole work too.

# Sample essays

All the historical topics are included in these sample essays, but they are intended to help you with essay writing and answering the question, rather than being about the specific content of the prescribed and related repertoire. Study all the essays thoroughly whether or not they are on a topic you have covered.

## QUESTION 1

### Compare the expressive use of harmony and tonality in the songs of Schumann and one other Lieder writer of the early nineteenth century. Refer to at least two songs by each composer.

Read this essay, making notes on its good points, but also mentioning ways in which it could have been improved. Then read the examiner's comments that follow.

Schumann and Schubert were the most important lieder composers of the early 19th century. They both used harmony and tonality to good effect in their songs.

In the first song from Schumann's Dichterliebe 'Im wunderschönen monat mai' a C# is held over an inverted chord of B minor moving to C#$^7$ in bar 2. This uncertainty of key foreshadows the uncertainty of the Poet's love. The music never settles with a perfect cadence in the key of F# minor suggested by the key signature, and several of the short vocal phrases sound unresolved. The postlude uses the chords of the opening, ending on an unresolved dominant 7th.

In contrast, in 'Im Rhein, im heiligen Strome' (song 6), which is about the mighty river Rhine flowing past the great cathedral of Cologne, the music begins firmly in E minor with the voice low down and doubled in the bass of the piano. Although there is much more diatonic harmony in this song, there is also some more adventurous chromatic writing, particularly in the accompaniment between the second and third stanzas, and the augmented 6th chord resolving to the dominant on 'love' at the end of the poem.

The final song of the cycle 'Die alten bösen lieder' begins in C# minor and depicts the desire to bury the old wicked songs and dreams. The harmony of the first verse only uses primary chords in the tonic key. There are striking diminished 7th chords in bars 39 and 40, suggesting the casting of the coffin into the sea. The song ends with a long piano postlude in D♭ major gradually sinking into a perfect cadence repeated three times.

In 'Auf dem Flusse' from Schubert's Die Winterreise there is simple harmony in E minor to start with, but it changes key for the stillness of the river. It goes to the major when the Poet talks about his lover.

Schumann and Schubert both use harmony and tonality in an expressive way in their songs.

## EXAMINER COMMENTS

This essay begins well and the student is able to write in some detail about songs from *Dichterliebe*. The section on Schubert is very brief and mentions only one song, not the *two* required by the question. The essay would score around 16/25, not higher, as it does not fulfil the demands of the question.

## QUESTION 2

**Discuss the transformation of themes in the interpretation of subject matter in Berlioz's *Symphonie fantastique*.**

Compare the two answers and note down the differences between them in terms of organisation and musical detail given. Then read the examiner's comments which follow.

## ANSWER A

Berlioz wrote this symphony after seeing the English actress Harriet Smithson, whom he later married, perform in a Shakespeare play in Paris. He was overwhelmed by her and by Shakespeare, and decided to write his Symphonie fantastique based on the imagination.

An artist, thought to be Berlioz himself, is obsessed with a woman (Harriet Smithson) and each movement of the symphony has an idée fixe which shows how the artist is affected by Harriet.

In the first movement called 'Dreams' the idée fixe is played by the violin and flute in unison. It is 40 bars long.

In the second movement the artist sees her at a ball. The tune is in $\frac{3}{4}$ time like a waltz.

In the third movement the idée fixe has agitated dotted rhythms for the passion of the artist.

The fourth movement is about a march to the guillotine because the artist has killed his beloved. The idée fixe stops when his head is cut off.

There are witches in the last movement and the idée fixe is played in a grotesque, distorted way on the clarinet.

This shows how Berlioz transforms the themes in his Symphonie fantastique.

# ANSWER B

Berlioz includes a very detailed programme for the 'Symphonie fantastique'. It is set in an opium inspired dream and shows how an artist is obsessed by a woman represented by the musical theme the idée fixe. The theme represents the artist's beloved and is transformed in each of the five movements according to the context in which he finds her in the dream. I am going to discuss the first appearance of the idée fixe in the first movement and its use in the 4th and 5th movements, together with other themes that are transformed in the work.

The idée fixe first appears allegro at b. 72 in C major (Quote 1) after a long slow introduction. It begins monophonically in the flute and violin and is over 40 bars long. It has irregular phrasing and the melody continually falls back onto F–E forming a semitone sigh which is a feature of this theme and throughout the work. The section is marked 'agitated and passionate' and the rest of the strings show this by their increasingly insistent interjections under the legato melody as it rises towards its climax.

The fourth movement is the March to the Scaffold in which the artist dreams he has killed his beloved and is sent to his execution. The first subject is a falling scale of G minor on cellos and basses in menacing march-like rhythm. This is heard in inversion and with a countersubject added as the march builds up to a tutti which features the brass. The only appearance of the idée fixe is as the artist thinks of his beloved for the last time. Only the first four bars are heard, at b. 164 in G major (Quote 2) poignantly played on unaccompanied C clarinet. The melody is cut off by a dramatic tutti G minor chord representing the fall of the guillotine.

The Dream of a Witches' Sabbath which forms the final movement sees the artist among a ghastly crowd of spirits, sorcerers and monsters gathered for his funeral. The idée fixe is heard again, now vulgar, trivial and grotesque. Heard first in C major on C clarinet and then, after an outburst from the orchestra, in E♭ major (Quote 3) on the shrill E♭ clarinet joined by piccolo, it is now in $\frac{6}{8}$ time with ornaments adding to its distorted nature and completely contrasting with its initial appearance as a beautiful melody in the first movement.

This is soon followed by bells tolling the death knell which leads to a statement of the Dies Irae plainchant melody from the requiem mass. Heard first in long note values (Quote 4) on low bassoons and ophicleides, the rhythm is then halved in horns and trombones and played in quaver/crotchet rhythm in woodwind and pizzicato strings.

In conclusion Berlioz transforms a number of themes in Symphonie fantastique, predominantly of course the idée fixe, but also other main themes and finally in the last movement the Dies Irae theme which would have been well known to his audience.

## EXAMINER COMMENTS

It is immediately evident that Answer A is much weaker than Answer B. Answer A spends too much time on background information and gives only a very brief comment on each movement of the work. Answer B concentrates on just three movements, but writes about them in more depth and also incorporates discussion of other themes which are transformed in the work. Four short quotes are included, which would be written on manuscript paper in the examination. Notice that the student states the intention to consider only three movements during the essay introduction. Answer A would score in the region of 10/25 as it gives so little musical information. Answer B would benefit from a little more detail on the later use of the *Dies Irae* theme and the punctuation in the essay could be clearer. It would score around 22/25.

## QUESTION 3A

### Discuss how Korngold's music for *The Adventures of Robin Hood* enhances the dialogue and action.

Read Questions 3A and 3B and their answers together. Assume that these are the two essays answered in the examination by one student. Note down the strengths and issues of each with regard to essay construction. Then compare your notes with the examiner's comments which follow.

The main way in which Korngold's music enhances the dialogue and action in The Adventures of Robin Hood is by having themes for different characters and changing them depending on the action and mood. Korngold used different techniques to do this including re-orchestrating and re-harmonising and turning the themes into smaller motifs so that they could be repeated and developed. He used the same ideas in different themes, for example the leap of a minor 9th is added to 'Robin's Theme' for 'Robin's Fighting Theme', and is also a feature of Sir Guy's theme. This is important in the scene when they duel, where their themes are varied.

The 'March of the Merry Men' is the first theme in the title music. It features a melody in thirds in clear four-bar phrases and a bridge section featuring a melody in parallel 4ths and a whole-tone scale. The title music ends with a fanfare which leads into the first scene. In the 'Archery Tournament', the Merry Men theme is re-orchestrated with muted strings making a softer sound showing that Robin and his Merry Men are in disguise.

In the 'Attack on Sir Guy's Men' in Sherwood Forest scene, the 'March of the Merry Men' theme has prominent trills and bassoon doubling violins to make it more amusing. When the men jump down out of the trees there are descending scales in the violins and harp glissando.

This is how Korngold enhances the dialogue and action.

## Illustrate the use of transformation of themes in interpreting the dialogue and action in two films by different composers.

I am going to discuss Korngold's The Adventures of Robin Hood and Max Steiner's Gone with the Wind.

Both composers use leitmotifs for their characters. Korngold re-orchestrated and re-harmonised the themes and turned them into smaller motifs depending on the action and mood. 'Robin's Theme' has a leap of a minor 9th added to it in 'Robin's Fighting Theme', and this is also a feature of Sir Guy's theme.

The 'Merry Men' theme also appears in different ways. At the start of the film it is the first theme as a March. In the 'Attack on Sir Guy's Men' in Sherwood Forest, it includes the bassoon for comic effect. It is much softer when Robin and his Merry Men are in disguise during the Archery Tournament.

The most famous theme in Gone with the Wind is 'Tara's Theme'. It is the title music for the film and represents Scarlett O'Hara's home. After Rhett has left her at the end of the film, she hears voices in her head talking about Tara. The music uses a chorus without words to create a dream-like atmosphere. The theme gradually develops and modulates to the major key and is transformed into the full theme as she realises she must go home to Tara.

Transformation of themes was important in early film music as it helped explain the dialogue and action to the audience.

## EXAMINER COMMENTS

The answer to Question 3A has some detail, but only addresses the themes used for some of the characters, not any other aspects of how the music enhances the dialogue and action. It would score around 14/25 as the examples lack range. The problem with the answer to Question 3B is that it duplicates almost all the material on Korngold from the first essay. The section on Steiner also lacks musical detail. The student could have chosen another composer instead of Korngold for the second essay, or could have considered different scenes or aspects of the music for the first essay. Because of the amount of duplication, which cannot be credited twice, this essay would only be awarded 8/25.

## QUESTION 4

## Explain Byrd's approach to harmony and tonality in his *Mass for Four Voices*. Refer to two movements in your answer.

Study the question carefully, and then read this essay, making notes on its good points, but also mentioning ways in which it could have been improved. Then read the examiner's comments which follow.

William Byrd (1543–1623) was the greatest English composer of the 16th century. He worked during the last great period of Catholic church music in England in the Elizabethan age. By the time he wrote this piece, Protestantism was established and Roman Catholics faced persecution. However, Byrd remained a Catholic and this was tolerated by the monarch.

Byrd wrote three masses, one in three parts, one in four parts and one in five parts. The mass is in five main sections, the Kyrie, Gloria, Credo, Sanctus and Agnus Dei.

The 'et resurrexit' section of the Credo begins in F minor and Byrd includes some high vocal ranges in the tenor and bass parts. These represent the words 'et ascendit in caelum' ('and ascended into heaven') and is an example of word painting. It is followed by a passage in faster rhythms in polyphony for 'sedet ad dexteram Patris' ('seated at the right hand of the Father'). Most of the end of the Credo is polyphonic and it ends with a melismatic 'Amen' which uses a major 7th suspension between the outer parts. The movement ends on an F major chord forming a tierce de Picardie.

## EXAMINER COMMENTS

There are several issues with this essay. The introduction is far too long and says nothing about the music. The student only considers the Credo, but two movements were required by the question. Most seriously, although on first reading the student seems to have quite good knowledge of the music, and its cultural and social context, only the very end of the essay mentions anything to do with harmony and tonality, which was the focus of the question. This would therefore score in the region of 10 or 11 marks out of 25.

## QUESTION 5

### Explain the use of vocal forces for dramatic effect in Purcell's *Dido and Aeneas*.

Read this essay, paying particular attention to its structure. Make notes on its good points, but also mention ways in which it could have been improved. Then read the examiner's comments which follow.

Purcell makes use of a variety of vocal forces in expressing his drama. Recitative, arias, duets and choruses are all important.

In 'Whence could so much virtue spring?' Dido's recitative, in which her love becomes evident, includes long melismas on 'storms', 'valour' and 'fierce'. This contrasts with the sighing repetition on the words 'how soft' with accented dissonance. The section is mainly in C minor with a brief move to F major for 'Venus' charms'. Belinda's response includes a chromatic Bb to B♮ expressive appoggiatura over a G major chord on 'woe'. Such dissonance was typical of English composers of the time and adds to the intense emotion of the drama.

The duet which follows, 'Fear no danger', for Belinda and the Second Woman is homophonic and sung in thirds. The music moves to C major giving a bright and cheerful effect after the long minor section. It is in a simple rondo form making use of a dance-like triple metre. The chorus then repeats the duet in four-part harmony, totally syllabic and homophonic, again in contrast to the preceding recitative and emphasising the changes of emotion seen in the drama.

In 'Come away', the First Sailor's melody uses unusual phrase lengths and includes the lombardic rhythm on 'never', this was typical of Purcell. The chorus of sailors then repeat the solo in a simple choral version which begins imitatively, but then becomes homophonic with the sopranos taking the melody.

## EXAMINER COMMENTS

This essay is generally well focused. There is a brief introduction and the student writes in some detail at the start, although the dramatic effect is not always explained. The last paragraph lacks depth and there is no conclusion. This would score in the region of 17/25. Perhaps the student could have included more examples if they had had time and the mark would probably then have been higher.

## QUESTION 6

**Discuss the effectiveness of the use of voice and accompaniment in at least three songs from *Not Too Late* by Norah Jones.**

Read this essay, paying particular attention to its structure. Make notes on its good points, but also mention ways in which it could have been improved. Then read the examiner's comments which follow.

Norah Jones uses different instrumental combinations in her songs and also uses different musical styles.

'Thinking About You' features a Hammond organ and Wurlitzer, and the song 'Not Too Late' uses a Mellotron – an electro-mechanical keyboard which can playback pre-recorded sounds.

'Thinking About You' has word painting such as the melisma on 'the leaves were falling down softly'.

'Wish I Could' is a strophic song with all six verses having the same music, but there is variety because of the changes of instrumentation.

In 'Wake Me Up' there is a syncopated guitar accompaniment with long sustained chords and pitch bending on the lap steel guitar, which gives a strong country feel.

'Wish I Could' uses a classical string sound for some of the verses and 'Broken' also uses string textures with pizzicato and bowed double bass and glissando on the cello.

'Sinkin' Soon' uses piano, trombone, bass, mandolin, drums, pots and pans, and a guitjo. The trombone uses blue notes and mutes. Blue notes also appear in the melody and Norah Jones makes a feature of these in her performance.

'My Dear Country' is traditional because it uses $\frac{3}{4}$ time like a waltz. It uses a range of diminished and augmented chords, but 'Broken' only uses a repeated chord pattern.

## EXAMINER COMMENTS

This essay demonstrates a complete lack of planning by the student. It reads as if they have just written everything they know in the order they thought of each point without any organisation of material or consideration of the requirement in the question to discuss the *effectiveness* of the use of voice and accompaniment. The question asks for at least three songs, but the student has written, seemingly at random, about aspects of seven songs. The student clearly has some specific knowledge of the music and it would have been much better to take time to plan the essay and to write about three songs in detail. This essay would only score about 10/25.

## EXERCISE

Consider all the essay titles in this section and, where appropriate, adapt them for work(s) in the topic you have studied. Write plans for each one and, if you have time, write the essay too.

# Further reading and listening

OCR A2 Music Study Guide (3rd Edition) by Huw Ellis-Williams and Gavin Richards published by Rhinegold Education has information on all the prescribed works and some related repertoire for each historical topic.

The Rhinegold Dictionary of Music in Sound by David Bowman has definitions of over 2,300 musical terms with scored and audio examples of each.

The BBC's Discovering Music series is a weekly radio programme discussing major works from the repertoire. Several of the prescribed works and some appropriate items of related repertoire have been featured over the years. Many of the discussions are still available on the BBC Radio 3 Discovering Music website.

Naxos Online Music Library (www.naxosmusiclibrary.com) contains a large number of recordings including works from the prescribed and related repertoire. Check if your school/ college or local public library subscribes to this.

# Glossary

**Absolute music**. Music that is not about anything other than itself.

**Aleatoric**. Music that has elements created by chance, for example the rolling of a die to generate rhythm for a melody.

**Anacrusis**. The note or notes that form an upbeat (or upbeats) to the first downbeat of a phrase.

**Antiphony**. A technique where two instrumental groups or two choirs alternate in dialogue.

**Appoggiatura**. An ornamental note that falls on the beat as a dissonance and then resolves by step onto the main note.

**Arpeggiando**. A performance direction found in string music in which the performer is instructed to interpret printed chords as arpeggios. In some Baroque music, an example of the arpeggiation will initially be written out as an example for the remaining bars.

**Articulation**. The manner in which a series of notes are played with regards to their separation or connection – for example, staccato (separated) or legato (connected).

**Atonal**. Western art music, which wholly or largely does not use keys or modes. Many early 20th-century composers saw atonality as the inevitable outcome of the perpetual chromaticism and modulation of some late Romantic music.

**Augmentation**. The lengthening of rhythmic values of a previously heard melody (for example in a fugue), or the widening of an interval.

**Auxiliary note**. A non-harmony note which is a step above (upper auxiliary) or below (lower auxiliary) the harmony note and returns to it.

**Avant-garde**. (French for 'vanguard') A label applied to composers considered to depart radically from accepted styles of composition.

**Ballett**. A light type of madrigal, popularised in England by Morley and Weelkes. Usually in triple time it can be distinguished by its fa-la-la refrains.

**Bariolage**. Rapid alternations between a recurring pitch on an open string and one or more pitches on an adjacent string.

**Binary form**. Two-part structure (AB), usually with both sections repeated.

**Bitonal/polytonal**. Bitonal music uses two different keys simultaneously; polytonal can refer to music using any number of keys greater than one. Clashing keys can be used to symbolise conflict in a drama for example in Britten's *Billy Budd*.

**Chord extension**. Chords which add additional 3rds to the third and fifth degree of a triad, creating a 7th, 9th, 11th or 13th. Although technically dissonant, chord extensions become more commonly used from the 19th century onwards. You will have encountered some of these in the instrumental jazz studied at AS level.

**Chromatic**. The use of non-diatonic notes (notes which are not in the current key). Chromatic notes or chromatic passages are often used for expressive purposes for example Bach's *St Matthew Passion*. In the 19th century, chromaticism played an increasing role for example in Wagner's *Die Walküre*.

**Circle of 5ths**. A series of chords whose roots are each a 5th lower (or a 4th higher) than the previous one. For example, Em–Am–Dm–G–C.

**Cluster**. A chord made up of adjacent notes.

**Col legno**. A string technique of playing with the wood of the bow.

**Compound metre.** Time signature in which the beat divides into, three: $\frac{6}{8}$, $\frac{9}{8}$, $\frac{12}{8}$.

**Con sordino**. An instruction to the performer to play with a mute.

**Consonant**. Intervals or chords which are stable and sound pleasant (for example, unisons, 3rds, 6ths), as opposed to its opposite, dissonant.

**Continuo**. Short for 'basso continuo', the continuo instruments form the accompaniment in Baroque music. It may include instruments such as the harpsichord (capable of playing full harmony) and a cello or bassoon reinforcing the bass line.

**Contrapuntal**. See Polyphonic.

**Contrary motion**. Movement of two parts in opposite directions to each other.

**Countermelody**. An independent melody which complements a more prominent theme.

**Cue**. A section or number from a film music score. Film music usually consists of a series of separately composed cues which can vary in length.

**Da capo aria**. Common aria form of Baroque opera and sacred music. ABA shape, with Da Capo instruction at the end of the B section. The singer may add ornamentation during the repeat.

**Diatonic**. Using notes that belong to the current key.

**Diegetic music**. Music in a film which forms part of the action (e.g. played or heard by one of the characters), not part of the underscore.

**Diminished 7th**. A four-note chord made up of a diminished triad plus a diminished 7th above the root.

**Dominant 7th**. A four-note chord built on the dominant (5th) note of the scale. It includes the dominant triad plus a minor 7th above the root.

**Double stopping**. A string technique of playing more than one string at a time. Also triple and quadruple stopping.

**False relation**. A chromatic contradiction between two notes sounded simultaneously and in different parts. For example a G natural against a G sharp.

**Falsetto**. This involves the singing of notes above the normal range of the human voice, normally by male singers.

**Galliard**. Lively Renaissance dance, popular in the Elizabethan Court, written in triple time.

**Gesamtkunstwerk**. (Ger. 'complete art work'). See Music drama.

**Glissando**. A slide between two notes.

**Ground bass**. Repeating bass, usually four or eight bars in length, with changing music in the other parts. Popular in Baroque music.

**Harmonic**. Sometimes known as flageolet note, a technique of lightly touching the string (e.g. on a violin) to produce a high, flute-like sound.

**Harmonic rhythm**. The rate at which harmony changes in a piece.

**Hemiola**. The articulation of two units of triple time (*strong-weak-weak, strong-weak-weak*) as three units of duple time (*strong-weak, strong-weak, strong-weak*).

**Hit point**. Point in a film score where the music coincides with an event in the action (sometimes known as 'catching the action').

**Homophonic**. A texture in which one part has a melody and the other parts accompany. In contrast to a polyphonic texture, in which each part has independent melodic interest.

**Imitation**. A contrapuntal device in which a distinct melodic idea in one part is immediately copied by another part, often at a different pitch, while the first part continues with other music. The imitation is not always strict, but the basic melodic and rhythmic outline should be heard.

**Leger line**. Additional lines used above or beneath the stave to represent notes that fall outside of its range.

**Leitmotif**. A theme which is associated with a character, situation, mood, object or idea, especially in the operas of Richard Wagner and dramatic works/film music of later composers.

**Libretto**. The script or words for a dramatic work which is set to music (e.g. an opera, musical or oratorio).

**Lombardic rhythm**. See 'Scotch Snap'.

**Masque**. Opera-like English court entertainment from the 17th and early 18th centuries.

**Mediant**. The third degree of a major or minor scale.

**Melisma**. A technique in vocal music, where a single syllable is set over a number of notes in the melody. Such a passage may be described as 'melismatic'.

**Metamorphosis**. Compositional device in minimalist music, aiming for gradual change achieved by altering one note of the previous chord at a time.

**Metric modulation**. A device for achieving a gradual change of tempo by setting a new beat which is a proportion of the previous beat.

**Middle-eight**. A passage that may be used in popular music forms, describing a section (usually consisting of eight bars and containing different music) that prepares the return of the main section.

**Minimalist**. A contemporary style of composing based on repetitions of short melodic and rhythmic patterns. Developed by American composers such as Steve Reich, Philip Glass and Terry Riley.

**Mode**. Seven-note scales that can be created using only the white notes of a piano keyboard. The dorian can be played beginning on D (i.e. D–E–F–G–A–B–C–D), the mixolydian on G, the aeolian on A and the ionian on C. These interval patterns can then be transposed to any other note. For example, dorian beginning on G (or G dorian) would be G–A–B♭–C–D–E–F–G.

The modes used in 16th-century church music came to interest later composers looking for an alternative to the major-minor tonal system. Often this was linked to a desire to imitate the sounds of church music or to use the modal styles of folksong to create a link with national identity for example, MacMillan's *The Confession of Isobel Gowdie*.

**Modulation**. The process of changing key. At AS level, modulation was usually to closely related keys. However, in the works studied for A2 you will see a more dramatic and expressive use of wide-ranging modulations, including keys which are distantly related. For example, Schumann's *Dichterliebe*.

**Monophonic**. A musical texture that uses a single melodic line.

**Multi-track recording**. A method of recording (normally for popular music) that allows sound sources to be recorded separately and later combined.

**Music drama**. Richard Wagner's term for his later operas, which attempted to combine music with the other arts to create a 'complete art work' (*Gesamtkunstwerk*).

**Obbligato**. Used in Baroque music to denote an instrumental solo part which must be included.

**Octatonic scale**. Literally an eight-note musical scale, this normally refers to a pattern of notes with alternating tones and semitones. Rimsky-Korsakov used it to exotic effect in *Scheherezade*.

**Ondeggiando (ondulé)**. A string technique of rapidly alternating between two strings.

**Ossia**. An alternative passage, normally written above the stave, that may be played instead of the original music. This may be an easier alternative in virtuosic operatic arias, for instance.

**Ostinato**. A repeated melodic, harmonic or rhythmic motif, heard continuously throughout part or the whole of the piece.

**Overdubbing**. A recording technique where an additional musical part is recorded to a previously recorded track. This technique is often used by pop musicians to create additional sounds and add more instruments to an existing recording.

**Pedal note**. A sustained or continuously repeated pitch, often in the bass, that is heard against changing harmonies. A pedal on the fifth degree of the scale (known as the dominant pedal) tends to generate excitement, while a pedal on the key note (known as the tonic pedal) tends to create a feeling of repose.

**Pentatonic**. A scale made up of five notes, most frequently the first, second, third, fifth and sixth degrees of a major scale (for example, C pentatonic is C–D–E–G–A).

**Phrasing**. In performance the execution of longer groups of notes which follow natural patterns of the music. 'Articulation' may be used to refer to phrasing over a shorter group of notes. Phrases may be indicated by the composer but the skill and judgement of the performer is also important in creating a successful performance.

**Plainchant**. Original monophonic music of the early Christian church.

**Polyphonic**. A texture consisting of two or more equally important melodic lines heard together. In contrast to a homophonic texture, in which one part has the melody and the other parts accompany. The term polyphonic has a similar meaning to contrapuntal, but is more often used for vocal rather than instrumental music.

**Portamento**. A slide between two notes.

**Power chord**. A term used in popular music to refer to a chord for guitar that omits the 3rd of the triad. It therefore contains a bare interval of a 5th.

**Programme music**. Music with a stimulus that comes from outside the music itself or depicts an extra-musical idea.

**Recitative**. A technique in opera and oratorio where the singer conveys the text in a speech-like manner. This is normally used to cover narrative effectively and contrasts with arias which are much more lyrical.

**Ritornello**. In Baroque music, the repeated tutti section used as a refrain; most often in the first or last movement of a concerto, or in arias or choral works.

**Ritornello form**. Standard form of first and last movements of the Baroque concerto, alternating tutti ritornelli with solo or ripieno (small group) sections.

**Rubato**. The alteration of rhythm, particularly in a melodic line, by lengthening and shortening notes but keeping an overall consistent tempo.

**Sacred music**. Music which is intended for worship or has a religious purpose.

**Scotch snap**. A two-note dotted rhythm which has the shorter note on the beat. Usually an on-beat semiquaver followed by an off-beat dotted quaver. Also known as lombardic rhythm.

**Secular music**. Music which does not have a religious purpose.

**Segue**. The continuation of one section or movement to another without a break. In popular albums, this refers to one track immediately following its predecessor.

**Sequence**. Immediate repetition of a melodic or harmonic idea at a different pitch, or a succession of different pitches.

**Serialism**. A system of composing atonal music, using a predetermined series of the 12 chromatic notes to guarantee equality of all pitches. For example, David Shire's jazz film score for *The Taking of Pelham One Two Three*.

**Skiffle**. A type of folk music with jazz and country influences. It also typically uses homemade or improvised instruments such as the comb and paper or kazoo.

**Sonata form**. Typical first movement form of the Classical and Romantic periods. In three sections – exposition, development, recapitulation – often based on two groups of melodic material in two contrasting keys (first subject, second subject).

**Sprechstimme**. A vocal technique which falls between speaking and singing.

**Strophic**. A song in which the music is repeated for each verse, for example a hymn.

**Sul ponticello**. A string technique of playing close to the bridge.

**Sul tasto**. A string technique of playing over the fingerboard.

**Symphonic poem**. Type of programme music for orchestra, depicting a character, mood or idea or telling a story. Also known as a Tone poem.

**Syncopation**. Placing the accents in parts of the bar that are not normally emphasised, such as on weak beats or between beats, rather than in the expected place on strong beats.

**Tabla**. A pair of hand-drums, used frequently in Indian Classical music performances.

**Temp track**. Temporary music track used in the early production of a film.

**Tessitura**. A specific part of a singer's or instrument's range. For example a 'high tessitura' indicates a high part of the range.

**Threnody**. (Greek thrēnos and ōidē) Wailing ode. A song of lament at a death.

**Through-composed**. A stage work (opera or musical) in which the music is not split into separate numbers. Also a song in which there is different music composed for each verse.

**Tierce de Picardie**. A major 3rd in the final tonic chord of a passage in a minor mode.

**Transcription**. The arrangement of a composition for other instruments (e.g. a piano version of an orchestral piece).

**Tritone**. An interval that is equivalent to three tones (an augmented 4th or dimished 5th).

**Underscore**. Music which accompanies or represents the action on screen without being part of it. Also used for instrumental music accompanying dialogue in a musical.

**Voicing**. The arrangement of pitches within a chord to create a particular texture.

**Whole-tone scale**. A scale in which the interval between every successive note is a whole tone.

**Word painting**. A technique of setting text in which the sound or movement implied by a word or phrase is imitated by the music (e.g. a falling phrase for 'dying').